"Y

For

retort that rose swiftly to her lips, but could think of nothing else to say. Besides, she didn't want to converse with Stoney Macreay. He'd always made her feel things she didn't understand.

She turned to her little girl. "Time to go, sweets," she said, and began guiding her to the car.

Stoney's hand on her arm stopped her. "I've been waiting to see you, Meredith. I'd like to talk with you about some things."

"Well, I have nothing to say to you. I've got my family to take care of me now." But her unspoken words were even clearer. *Leave Tess and me alone.*

She thought for a moment he was going to let her go, but he said instead, so low that she had to strain her ears to catch his words, "Families can't take care of *every* need."

Dear Reader,

Take one married mom, add a surprise night of passion with her almost ex-husband, and what do you get? *Welcome Home, Daddy!* In Kristin Morgan's wonderful Romance, Rachel and Ross Murdock are now blessed with a baby on the way—and a second chance at marriage. That means Ross has only nine months to show his wife he's a FABULOUS FATHER!

Now take an any-minute-mom-to-be whose baby decides to make an appearance while she's snowbound at her handsome boss's cabin. What do you get? *An Unexpected Delivery* by Laurie Paige—a BUNDLES OF JOY book that will bring a big smile.

When one of THE BAKER BROOD hires a sexy detective to find her missing brother, she never expects to find herself walking down the aisle in Carla Cassidy's *An Impromptu Proposal*.

What's a single daddy to do when he falls for a woman with no memory? What if she's another man's wife—or another child's mother? Find out in Carol Grace's *The Rancher and the Lost Bride*.

Lynn Bulock's *And Mommy Makes Three* tells the tale of a little boy who wants a mom—and finds one in the "Story Lady" at the local library. Problem is, Dad isn't looking for a new Mrs.!

In Elizabeth Krueger's *Family Mine*, a very eligible bachelor returns to town, prepared to make an honest woman out of a single mother—but she has other ideas for him....

Finally, take six irresistible, emotional love stories by six terrific authors—and what do you get? Silhouette Romance—every month!

Enjoy every last one,

Melissa Senate
Senior Editor

Please address questions and book requests to:
Silhouette Reader Service
U.S.: 3010 Walden Ave., P.O. Box 1325, Buffalo, NY 14269
Canadian: P.O. Box 609, Fort Erie, Ont. L2A 5X3

FAMILY MINE

Elizabeth Krueger

Silhouette
ROMANCE™
Published by Silhouette Books
America's Publisher of Contemporary Romance

This one's for Fred and Matt.

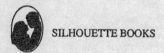

SILHOUETTE BOOKS

ISBN 0-373-19155-3

FAMILY MINE

Copyright © 1996 by Cheryl Krueger McGuire

Books by Elizabeth Krueger

Silhouette Romance

A Saving Grace #774
And the Walls Come Tumbling Down #798
His Father's House #872
Dark Prince #960
Family Mine #1155

Silhouette Special Edition

For the Children #723

ELIZABETH KRUEGER

left her home in Chicago to live on a small farm in northwestern Michigan when she married a widower with nine children. Thirteen years and four more children later, Elizabeth has successfully pursued a new career—writing. Perhaps her creativity has been inspired by the many lives she has guided and loved, or maybe her writing was her one escape from a household that at many times must have been impossibly chaotic. All we can be sure of is that her readers are her true beneficiaries.

All underlined places are fictitious.

Chapter One

The small crowd at the Colton High School soccer field was cheering wildly. Only two minutes into the game, and Colton had already scored their first goal. After all, it was not for nothing that Colton ranked first in the state of Indiana. There were ten experienced seniors on this team, and this year they had as their new coach Stoney Macreay.

Stoney Macreay. Meredith Blackmoore sat midway up the bleachers, her arm loosely wrapped around her daughter, Tess, and watched the coach shout instructions to his team. He hadn't seen her yet, but she knew their meeting was inevitable. This crowd wasn't large enough to lose herself in. She felt tense, strung out, and wished with all her heart she hadn't given in to her family and come here. The waiting was intolerable....

Down on the Colton bench, Meredith's brother, Roger, moved his body in little eager bounces, ready to go whenever the coach called him. He'd been getting quite a bit of playing time lately. He was one of Colton's up-

and-coming juniors, and already Stoney was moving Roger and several others more and more often into the games.

Meredith knew this because everyone in her family talked about it. A lot. Blackmoores always supported each other in their chosen endeavors. Which made her reluctance to attend any of Roger's games all the more obvious.

Not that Mom and Dad didn't understand. They did, only too well. "Stoney isn't his brother Tom," her mother had finally said. "And he isn't Tom's father, either. He's always been polite to us, and he's showed no prejudice to Roger. You ought to go, honey. Instead of hiding away."

"You've nothing to be ashamed of," her father had added gruffly. "This is a small town. You'll have to see Stoney Macreay sometime. Go to a game and get it over with."

But her mother and father didn't know everything, she thought darkly. Still, in the end she had allowed herself to be convinced.

Mom and Dad were here, of course. They were sitting with Roger's girlfriend, Beth, three rows down and to the right. Mom, wearing a bright red cardigan, was calling out encouragement to the entire Colton team. Dad was standing, his hands shielding his eyes from the brilliant Indiana sun, waiting with enthusiasm to equal Roger's for the coach to call his son into the game.

Three more minutes passed. Colton scored another goal. They were outshooting the other team three to one. Coach Macreay called up Roger and another boy named Adam Brown to enter play.

Roger sprang forward. Running in place, he waited for the buzzer to give him permission to enter the field.

"That's Uncle Roger," Tess said excitedly. "See—he's number fifteen! He's going to play now, Mommy." Tess clapped her hands. "I hope he scores a point!"

"Me too, sweetie," Meredith said. "Let's keep our fingers crossed for him, okay?"

Meredith's eyes wandered down to the left. Sitting alone, looking perfectly poised and supremely sure of herself, was Stoney's latest blond bombshell. She'd been dropped off by someone driving a little yellow roadster, just minutes before the game was to start. Meredith had watched the blonde get Stoney's attention, then blow him a luxuriant kiss. Stoney had grinned appreciatively before turning back to his boys.

But Meredith didn't have to see this little exchange to know who the woman was. It was the long feathered hair that gave her away. And the total makeup job for an afternoon of high school game-watching. And the skin-tight stretch pants, accompanied by a deep blue blouse that opened just enough to reveal the beginnings of an overripe bosom.

She was Stoney's, all right.

The blonde looked just like all the other women Stoney had draped over his body for as long as Meredith could remember. When he had played soccer for State U. and had dated one of the cheerleaders, for instance. And afterward, when he had been the star forward of the Black Knights, for whom he had played professional soccer for six brilliantly triumphant years.

Stoney Macreay had been the news media's baby. He was the golden boy who had it all—all the money, all the success, all the romance. And if he sometimes had a flaring temper and a cruel wit—well, those things also made for scintillating press.

Then, at the end of last season, Stoney had fallen hard and been kicked—not on purpose, everyone swore. But his right kneecap was fractured and the ligaments all up

and down his right thigh were torn badly. Stoney Macreay's professional life as a soccer player was over. With
his manager at his side, he had solemnly announced his
premature retirement before a huge crowd of weeping
fans.

Weeping.

Meredith rolled her eyes. Jocks. They were all alike.
The heroes of society. She wouldn't give a plugged nickel
for any of them.

"Look, Mommy! Look! Roger's running with the
ball! He's going to kick it in! Mommy! Watch!" Tess had
jumped up on the bench behind her and was practically
screaming in her ear.

But the opposing goalie caught the ball. Meredith saw
her brother mouth some words at the goalie, and the
other player's face darkened in sudden rage. Smirking,
Roger turned and ran downfield with the rest of his team
to receive the kick.

Roger played for about five more minutes before he
was called back to the bench. Meredith had to admit her
family was right—he was a darned good player for
someone just up from the JV ranks. But that moment at
the net bothered her, even though such behavior was
probably just part of the game. Still, she remembered
other times lately when Roger had been sullenly rude and
quick to anger.

Maybe it was just male hormones.

She was glad her only child was a girl. No testosterone
to deal with there. All the PMS in the world couldn't
equal a teenage boy's aggressive drive.

The halftime whistle sounded. Colton led, three to
nothing. Stoney's blond knockout stood and stretched
sinuously, like a bored, well-fed cat. As the boys came in
off the field, Stoney absentmindedly turned and sur-
veyed the small group of fans.

Colton was a traditional town. Football in the fall. Basketball in the winter. Baseball in the spring. Even with Stoney Macreay coaching, soccer was still not a big draw. Most of the people here today were friends and family of the players. These kids played for the love of the game, not for local adulation.

Men and their games, Meredith thought sarcastically. They start young and never grow up.

She wondered if Stoney missed the bright lights. She'd been surprised and dismayed when he had announced his intention to come back to his hometown and spend a year or so coaching a Class B team. Especially since she knew his family was no longer here. Just as the thought was thinning her mouth into a tight line, Stoney's casual gaze passed her by.

Then stopped. Narrowed. Returned to her face, and stayed. And even from this distance, she saw something indefinable flicker in the shadowed depths of his gaze. Something that said he'd been waiting for this moment as much as she had been avoiding it.

The sun was at his back, surrounding his gold-streaked head with a halo of light, his features shaded so that the dominant angles of his face—beloved by photographers everywhere—were momentarily softened. He didn't move, didn't smile, didn't nod. He just stood there, watching her as if he had all the time in the world. Waiting for her to react.

It was too late now to look away, to pretend she hadn't really seen him. She could only stare distantly back, her chin raised and her eyes cold, doing her best to deny the recognition and memories sizzling between them like a suddenly live wire. Tess jumped down from the bench above, and instinctively Meredith surrounded her daughter with a protective arm. Some of her tension must have communicated itself to Tess, because the child became quickly and uncustomarily still.

Stoney shifted and broke the contact. Deliberately his gaze traveled to Tess, took in her dark brown hair, her little upturned nose, her lithe young body encased in jeans and T-shirt. He stared at Meredith's daughter a long time, his face an expressionless mask.

Abruptly Meredith turned to Tess, making a show of buttoning her child's fall jacket. She was dismayed to find she was trembling slightly. "Would you like to go play on the swing set, honey?" she said. There was a family playground just south of the soccer field; several young children, bored with the game, were there already.

"I'd rather stay and watch Uncle Roger."

"Look. There's Suzy. And Nicole. And it's halftime. Why don't you go play?"

For a moment Tess stood, indecisive. Then, with the blitheness of youth, she said, "All right. I'll be back soon, though. To watch Roger." Then she ran off.

When Meredith returned her attention to the field, Stoney was huddled with his team, his outstretched arm punctuating some point he was making. Roger, his body never completely still, was listening intently.

Roger's girlfriend, Beth, rose and made her way to Meredith's side.

Beth Pierson was just about the prettiest sixteen-year-old in Colton, Meredith thought. She was a nice girl, too—quiet and, until she got to know you, kind of shy.

"Wow!" Beth said. "Did you see the way Coach Macreay stared at you?"

No, Meredith thought wryly. I missed it entirely.

"Did he?" she said with apparent uninterest.

"Yeah. And look at the blonde. She appears a little green, if you ask me."

Meredith couldn't help herself. She turned and looked.

The woman was glaring daggers at her. The blonde's perfectly made-up eyes were contracted in angry speculation; her pouty lips rude and hard looking. Impulsively Meredith gave her a wide, innocently friendly smile. The woman flounced and turned away.

"It's all right," Meredith said under her breath. "You can have him, honey."

"What?" Beth asked.

Meredith stood. "Nothing," she said dismissively.

"Do you and Coach know each other?"

"We've met once or twice. A long time ago."

"Umm—"

"Look. I'm going to sit by Mom. You want to come with me?"

"In a minute. I think I'll get a hot chocolate or something."

"See you in a few, then."

"Okay, Meredith," Beth said. "See you."

Well, Meredith thought, stepping down the bleachers to the empty space by her mother. So it happened. They'd seen each other, she and Stoney. It hadn't been such a big deal, after all. The earth hadn't quaked; the heavens remained closed. Nothing had changed.

So Meredith told herself, and she tried to believe it. She tried to believe it so hard that the entire second half passed in a blur. Late in the game Roger scored a goal, and she wouldn't even have noticed except for the fact that her parents, Tess and Beth were all standing screaming their heads off. Then the game was over. Colton won, of course. Seven to nothing. Afterward Roger came running up to where his family was waiting.

"Fine job, son," Meredith's father said, giving Roger a big bear hug. "Great goal you scored."

"You played marvelously," her mother added.

"Wonderful game, Uncle Roger!" Tess squealed.

Meredith merely smiled. It was obvious that Roger was only half paying attention, anyway. As soon as he could, he turned from his folks and lifted Beth down out of the stands. "Congratulations, Rog," Meredith heard Beth say breathlessly before her brother wrapped his arm around his girlfriend and kissed her deeply.

There was a moment of shocked silence. "Roger!" Meredith's father remonstrated. Roger raised his head, but instead of looking shamefaced or embarrassed, he seemed on the verge of real anger. Then his young face went deliberately still, almost sullen. He patted Beth's rear with a studied familiarity that bordered on insolence. "See you tonight?" he said.

Beth's face was flaming red. She gave Roger a jerky nod. "Sure, Rog," she said before throwing Meredith's parents a quick apologetic look and scurrying off to her car.

Meredith's mom urged, "You'd better have a talk with that boy!" and her dad nodded, his expression troubled.

Meredith turned to see Stoney's blonde move with languid grace onto the field. Almost absentmindedly Stoney put his arm around her waist. It was a careless enough gesture, but it was all the encouragement the woman needed to snuggle up disgustingly close. "Stoney, honey," Meredith heard her say, "I haven't seen you in *weeks*." Then the blonde reached up and pulled his head down for a kiss. Just as Stoney was moving to accommodate her, he looked up and saw the hard cynicism in Meredith's face.

She sensed his sudden stillness. His eyes took on that waiting look again, even as something hot and somehow accusatory burned in their depths. For some reason Meredith felt suddenly guilty, like a Peeping Tom. She drew in a breath. It wasn't her fault they were all over each other, on public display. At least the blonde was all over *him*, anyway. Meredith refused to look away.

His right eyebrow rose. His mouth lifted in a mirthless smile. He looked down at the curvaceous sweet thing at his side and lowered his head, giving the woman the kiss she was demanding. And a good, long kiss it was, too.

"Meredith," her mom said, fretting. "Don't stare, for goodness' sake."

Meredith's face went red. For a minute she had forgotten there was anyone else around. She had forgotten where she *was*. She sat down with a hard plump on the bleacher seat.

"We're going," her mom said. "We'll take Roger. Why don't you stay and play with Tess?"

"I have to go back to work, Mom," Meredith said.

"Right away?" the older woman asked in dismay. "It's Saturday afternoon, and you've already put in God knows how many hours this week. Your daughter needs you, Meredith."

"Kathleen!" Meredith's dad said sharply. "What Meredith has to do, she has to do. We'll take care of Tess."

But Tess had already run back to the swing set, where her little-girl legs were pumping her high in the sky. "Can I stay, Mommy?" she called out, begging. "Pleeaase?"

"I'll let her play a few minutes," Meredith said slowly. "I'll stay and play with her for a while."

"You don't have to, Merry," her dad said quietly.

"Yes, I do," she said. "Mom's right, Dad. Tess is growing up fast. I need to spend more time with her. I can work later, after she's in bed." She forced a smile. "You guys go on. Tess and I'll be fine. *I'll* be fine."

She waved her family off. She loved her parents dearly and was often overwhelmed with gratitude for what they'd done for her, but sometimes she wished . . .

A picture formed itself in her head. Of herself on a college campus. Studying. Learning. Of a house, white with blue shutters. Not large, but her own. Of a husband, sharing her dreams with her. Of a family—her own—separate from her parents.

She gave a wistfully small, defiant toss to her head. Maybe someday those things would be hers. But for now she was lucky to have all she did. It was too stupid to feel sorry for herself, and she wouldn't do it. Unconsciously she straightened her shoulders and went to play with Tess.

Only she really didn't do much playing. She sat on a park bench and watched Tess leave the swings to go rough-and-tumble through a jungle gym. Her daughter certainly had a lot of energy. Tough, wiry little arms and legs, always reaching out for something to do, to climb on, to jump over.

From where she was sitting, she could just see the parking lot. The rest of the fans were packing up and going home. Out of the corner of her eye she watched Stoney open the door to his sports car so his lady friend could slide in. He walked around to the other side and got in himself. His car engine roared to life. She waited for him to drive away.

But he didn't go anywhere. He let the car idle for a moment. He turned and said something to his girlfriend. Then he cut the engine and got back out, walking to where Meredith sat in solitary silence on the bench.

She closed her eyes briefly and clenched her fists. She straightened her back and lifted her chin. It didn't take him long to arrive at a spot next to her, yet she did nothing to acknowledge his presence. She felt him look at her, felt him wait to speak as if he were weighing his words.

"I'd like to talk with her," he said at last.

"No."

Tess, however, had other plans. The child looked over from her position atop a tall slide, and immediately came whooshing down.

"Hey!" Tess said. "You're the coach!"

"That's right." Stoney hunkered down on his ankles so he could meet Tess's eyes.

"My uncle plays on your team."

"I know." His mouth quirked upward in a smile.

"He made a score today!"

Stoney's smile grew broader. "I know that, too."

"This is my mommy."

Stoney looked at Meredith, slow and easy. His eyes appeared as they always had to her—stormy and deep. "We've met."

Meredith stood, gathering her purse.

He inclined his head. "Your mother and I are old friends."

For Tess's sake she swallowed the acid retort that rose swiftly to her lips, and said merely, "Congratulations on the win, Stoney."

"Thanks. The boys played well." He rose, stretching his body upward like the lion she once thought he was.

She didn't say anything else. Small talk was never easy for her—she'd become an adult too soon for that. Besides, she didn't want to converse with Stoney Macreay. He'd always made her feel things she didn't understand. His eyes on her face brought a rising warmth in her cheeks; she knew she was blushing. She looked away, at her daughter.

"Time to go, Tess," she said. "Run and get in the car, sweets."

"Aw, Mom. Do I *have* to?"

"Yes. Now. Go on."

"Meredith—" Stoney began.

"Bye, Coach," Tess said, running obediently to the car.

"Gotta go, Stoney," Meredith said. "Maybe I'll see you around. At Roger's games."

Stoney didn't move. In order to get to her car, she had to walk by him. She took a couple of steps before he grasped her arm, tight. To an observer—to the blonde in the car—it would have been a deceptively casual gesture. But his fingers bit into her skin, and his eyes, turned toward Meredith, were suddenly blazing.

Meredith met his gaze, saying nothing. After a while she looked pointedly at his hand upon her arm. He didn't let go.

"She doesn't look much like Tom, does she?" he said.

Meredith's head snapped up. "No," she replied, giving a light, scornful laugh. "Which I'm sure would be a great relief to him. If he'd ever seen her, that is."

"Tom's married now," Stoney said carefully.

"Oh?"

"Two years ago. They have a kid. A boy."

Actually she hadn't thought about Tom in a long time. The thought of him was an intrusion now. "Fine," she said with deceptive calm. Then she repeated, "Time for me to go, Stoney."

If anything, his grip on her arm grew tighter. "I've been waiting to see you, Meredith. I'd like to talk with you about some things."

"You're not involved," she said. "And I've got nothing to say."

He laughed low, under his breath. "Tom was a bastard, Meredith. And a fool to give you up. I'm sorry for what he did to you."

She kept her head up as she met his eyes. She felt very cool now. Very cool and distant. "I've got Tess," she said. "I'm not sorry." Then she added, "But I do want to be left alone, Stoney Macreay. Totally alone."

Something in his eyes changed then, and she felt a little ragged breath catch in her throat. "Alone," he repeated flatly. Then he shook his head. "I've tried that, Meredith." As if he couldn't help himself, his gaze moved slowly and with almost unwilling deliberation to her lips.

She sucked in her breath tightly. How long had it been since she'd been looked at like that? Something in her stirred, but she clamped it down. "You've got a willing body sitting in the car over there, remember, Macreay?" she made herself say, giving a thin-lipped smile.

She was surprised by the warm rush of color that suffused his cheeks. "Right," he said lightly. "Too true. I've got women all over me. All the time. Is that what you're thinking, Meredith?"

"Yes." Her answer was steady. "And I'm thinking some other things, Stoney. Like you don't need me. And Lord knows I don't need you. I've got family. We—all of us—take care of our own."

His eyes seemed to shutter themselves against her. "You're all right, then. Things are all right."

"Yes," she said.

She said nothing else, but her unspoken words were clear: *Leave Tess and me alone, Stoney Macreay.*

She thought for a minute he was going to let her go, but he said instead, so low that she had to strain her ears to catch his words, "Families can't take care of *every* need, Meredith Blackmoore."

His arrogance took her breath away. She felt suddenly naked and vulnerable. She said the first thing that came into her head, regretting her defensive cruelty even as she spoke, "How would you know?"

He went still then, absorbing the knife she had driven into his heart. His eyes never strayed from her face.

"I'm sorry," she whispered. "That was..."

"True," he said bitterly. "You never were a liar, Meredith."

"Please let me go."

He stared at her a moment longer, then released her arm. She turned away from him, walked with proud grace to where Tess was waiting in her old sedan, and—without one backward glance—headed home.

*   *   *

Stoney stalked around the hood of his high-priced sports car. He jerked open the door and flung his body into the driver's seat, slamming the door shut behind him. He sat with his hands gripping the steering wheel, staring wrathfully out the window.

Damn her. Damn her cool young beauty and her clear, honest eyes.

He thought of the child. Tess, she had called her. A pretty name. He remembered the way she had talked about her Uncle Roger.

His face darkened. He was also Tess's uncle. And he wanted the child to know it.

He may not know much about families, but he knew enough to understand that in a normal world, fathers didn't abandon their children, grandparents didn't deny their grandchildren and uncles were a part of their nieces' lives.

Normal. Hell.

Besides, it was clear enough that Meredith hadn't changed. She didn't want—

"Stoney, honey." The intentionally husky, sensuous female voice brought him back to harsh reality. "Remember me, darling?"

For one brief second Stoney felt absurd, inane. The sudden emptiness in his gut was all too familiar—it happened to him more and more frequently since he'd quit being a pro. Hell, it had happened before that.

He stretched his arm out along the leather bucket seat and turned to Karen. "Sorry, sweetheart," he said, at least half meaning it.

"Who is she?" Karen was studying her perfectly manicured nails.

He didn't pretend to misunderstand. "The sister of one of my players."

"You know her before?"

"Yeah," he admitted. "A little."

Karen shifted. She hated being ignored. For a second he caught a flash of feline fury in her eyes. "More than a little, Stoney," she drawled.

Stifling a sigh, he put his hand around Karen's silken neck, using his thumb to rub the little hollow that was one of her unique pleasure points. He didn't think the action out—he just automatically did what was necessary to distract Karen from asking so many damned questions. He hated people who asked questions. If you answered them you had to reveal yourself, and that was something Stoney never did.

Karen closed her eyes and made a little throaty sound that was more drama than spontaneous reaction. "She's not your type," she purred.

That was the truth. Even six years ago, when she'd been barely sixteen, Meredith Blackmoore had been way out of his league.

Too bad his brother Tom hadn't felt the same way.

Karen pouted. He'd been thinking of other things, and his hand had stilled upon her neck. She turned to him now, her mouth as full and inviting as the damned magazine model she wanted to be. She'd even had collagen implanted in her lips.

Fake lips, he thought. Fake moans. Fake love. Fake life. It wasn't all in his past, as he'd hoped. Even in Colton he hardly knew what was real.

"Stoney." If possible, those lips got poutier.

Too bad he'd never felt less like kissing them. Still, Stoney knew what was expected. He'd always known. He leaned over and put his mouth against hers. Karen put her hand high on his leg. The one where all his muscles and tissues were torn to kingdom come. "Stoney," she said again, this time lowering her voice to an inviting whisper.

He pulled away, effectively hiding his sudden distaste. He started the engine, felt the power of the sports car surge into life. Karen's hand was still on his thigh. Her lips stayed in their perpetual pout.

But as they drove down the road to the house he'd rented, Stoney wasn't thinking about Karen's full lips or the hand that was squeezing the muscles of the leg that was never going to work the way it should again. He wasn't thinking of Karen at all.

He was thinking about lovely dark-haired Meredith Blackmoore.

He knew what she expected—she expected him to leave her alone.

But for once in his colorful life, Stoney Macreay wasn't going to live up to someone else's expectations. He was going to do what he wanted, and to hell with the consequences.

Besides, Meredith hadn't always preferred to be alone. There was a time when she had belonged to his brother.

And as he drove the rest of the way to his house, Stoney Macreay wondered fiercely whom she belonged to now.

Chapter Two

It took Meredith less than ten minutes to drive to her parents' home. She and Tess went in the back door. Meredith's mother was in the kitchen, preparing the evening meal. Her mother had discarded the red sweater and had a big I'm The Boss apron tied around her waist.

"We're here," Meredith said, grinning as Tess ran off to find her grandfather.

"Dinner's almost ready." Her mother's face softened as she, too, watched Tess.

"I'll be right back." Meredith headed for her bedroom. "Save the table for me—I'll set it."

The Blackmoore house was one of the largest in Colton. It sat on a hill, overlooking the farms on the east, the town on the west. Meredith and Tess had adjoining bedrooms on the second floor. Her father had made the space over into a kind of suite, and the bathroom across the hall was considered their private property.

Meredith was no fool; she recognized her good fortune. When she'd had Tess, unmarried, three months before her seventeenth birthday, her parents had stood by her. They hadn't wasted any time with recriminations or accusations, but had simply gone about the task of preparing their daughter for motherhood and readying their home for a grandchild. Often in the past six years, Meredith thought about other young girls, pregnant and unwed as herself, but without family or friends to guide them. Sometimes it scared her, how lucky she'd been.

Because even with a loving family, it hadn't been easy. For a long time she'd been in a state of suspended disbelief. That one groping, drunken night in the back seat of a car could have produced such an astounding result as *pregnancy* made her feel not only lost and out of control, but also deeply ashamed. There hadn't even been any *love* involved. The whole thing had happened so fast that she hardly knew the end from the beginning. Date rape took on new meaning to her, and yet if she'd been asked, she would have been hard put to say it had been rape at all.

It had just been . . . fumbling. And a little pain. And a whole lot of embarrassment.

Surely a baby couldn't come from *that*.

But it had. Tess had. And Meredith's life had been changed forever. . . .

Two months shy of her sixteenth birthday, local football hero Tom Macreay had surprised Meredith by calling her up and asking her to a movie. She barely knew Tom—after all, he was a senior and she only in her second year. Besides, he was the school big shot, the boy every girl wanted. The guys he hung out with were all tough-guy jocks, and the girls who made it within his charmed circle were all popular and pretty. His prowess on the football field was constantly being celebrated in the local papers, and Meredith knew he was being scouted by several colleges. And he was handsome, in a rugged, athletic kind of way—thick blond hair, an almost shy, lopsided smile, broad, muscular shoulders.

He made all the girls swoon.

To top it off, Tom was the younger brother of soccer great Stoney Macreay. People all across the country were learning *that* name, and it was inevitable that in a small town like Colton, even though their sports were not the same, Tom caught a lot of his brother's reflected glory.

Yes indeed, Tom Macreay was big news in Colton.

So that his request for a date—when it came—was a complete shock. Meredith, studious and shy, never dreamed of moving within Tom Macreay's circle of friends. The closest she'd got to him was sharing a first-semester class, when Tom sat across the aisle from her. While they hardly said two words to each other, Tom told her later that she intrigued him even then.

She'd stuttered with shyness when he called. "My—my parents want me to wait until I'm sixteen to go out," she finally managed to say.

On the other end of the phone, Tom was silent. Then he said, "You mean, you've never even *been* on a date?"

"No," she admitted, feeling foolish and unsophisticated. "My parents are kind of traditional...."

"Couldn't you make up some story, tell them you're spending the night with a girlfriend?" Tom asked.

"I don't *lie,*" she said, finding it was possible to feel indignant and terribly excited at the same time.

"Ask them, then," he urged. "You're almost sixteen now. See if they'll let up."

And—surprisingly—her parents did.

"You've been absolutely no trouble to us," her father said indulgently. "I think we can trust you with this."

Her mother was more reserved. "I wouldn't normally agree, but you're going to be sixteen soon anyway," she said. "I guess there's no point in being rigid."

If only they had been, Meredith thought later. Two months would have made all the difference in the world. Tom would never have waited—he would have found someone else by then.

But how could they have known? How could *she* have known? Her parents agreed, and Meredith, thrilled to be the chosen of Tom Macreay, told him she could go.

At first their dates were circumspect. School dances. More movies. Even a picnic. Tom told Meredith she was the prettiest girl he'd ever seen, that he'd noticed her for a long time. He loved the fact that he was her first boyfriend, he said. He was glad she was a star student— maybe all those brains would rub off on him. He found the idea of quiet, beautiful, brainy Meredith Blackmoore sitting in the stands watching his games unbearably exciting. He played for *her,* he whispered. *She* was his inspiration.

Such dumb lines. She knew that now. Hard to believe that for such a long time she had trusted every one of them.

It wasn't long before Tom was pressing her to go to other events besides movies and games and high school dances. On the weekends, mostly, at friends' houses where the parents never seemed to be home. "Let's stop just for a minute," he'd say. "Everyone goes. What can it hurt?"

Indeed. What, or perhaps more accurately, *who?*

The parties were like nothing Meredith had ever seen: unrestrained behavior accompanied the kegs of beer and innumerable joints of pot. Sometimes other things were passed around—condoms, pills, powder. People came and went, freely using the front door, other times disappearing into back bedrooms. Still, Meredith was humiliatingly slow on the uptake—it took her a long time to figure out what was going on in the dark, unchaperoned bedrooms. People she *knew,* for goodness' sake. And not always with the same partners.

It was a different type of education than she had previously received, and one for which she had been ill prepared.

Almost immediately Tom had become impatient with the strict curfew her parents set. "Why can't they let you grow up?" he asked her more than once. His kisses became more demanding, his embraces more intimate. He began to drink when he was with her. Beer mostly, which made him mellow. Malt liquor, which made him silly. And straight vodka, which made him totally unpredictable.

"But you're in *training,*" Meredith remonstrated once.

"If you won't tell," Tom said, grinning, "I won't, either."

The changes Tom Macreay made in Meredith's life were so great that she could hardly think straight. She suspended judgment on everything, and quit making her own decisions. She learned to pretend that everything was normal, and hid her own deep confusion. Privately she was ashamed that she didn't enjoy Tom's kisses more, so she pretended that she did. What she saw and heard and felt of the high school nightlife of Colton was too shocking for words, but no one else seemed affected, so she pretended she wasn't, either. Everyone seemed in awe of her now that she was Tom Macreay's girlfriend, and while her sudden popularity didn't exactly bring happiness, it did make her giddy; at sixteen it was easy to pretend that giddiness and happiness were the same thing.

Then Tom's big brother, Stoney, came home for a weekend visit from his final year at State U. He offered his brother a double date.

"You're dating Tom Macreay *and* going double with Stoney?" Meredith's friend Joy said dreamily. "You must feel like a *princess*, Merry. Like Cinderella or something.''

And because that's the way her best friend defined her, Meredith decided that was exactly how she felt. An almost-sixteen-year-old princess.

''Wear something sexy,'' Tom demanded. ''I don't want you looking like a baby tonight.''

Meredith didn't own anything sexy. But she did have a tight-fitting night blue dirndl-style jumper that buttoned up the front. Usually she wore a snowy white lacy blouse with it, but tonight she daringly left the blouse off. The only problem was her bra straps showed when she moved her shoulders; taking a deep breath for courage, she removed her bra, too. She knew her parents would disapprove; she covered herself with a jacket so they wouldn't notice. And to appease both them and her own conscience, she deliberately went light on her makeup. Although she told herself as she did so, I'm grown-up now. I can do what I want.

Which didn't explain why she was a bundle of nerves that night when Tom called for her. He looked exceptionally handsome in his dark blue blazer and gray pants. His hair was combed back neatly; he was freshly shaved. Best of all, she noted with relief that he appeared sober, although with Tom sometimes it was hard to tell. His brother Stoney wasn't with him. He walked with her with his smooth athlete's pace to his car.

Immediately things started going wrong. Her relief was short-lived; he wasn't sober at all.

''I had to bring my own wheels,'' he said, his resentment openly bright and mocking, ''because of your curfew. Stoney and his date will probably be out all night, having *real* fun.''

Tom pulled a bottle of vodka from the pocket of his car door. ''Want some?'' he asked.

Her stomach wrenched. "Why do you have to drink that, Tom?" she said. "You know it makes you..." Her voice faded away when she saw the quickly growing rage in his eyes.

"Makes me what?" Tom asked dangerously.

"Different," she said quietly, intuitively using her voice and manner to calm him. She felt better when he seemed to subside a little.

He shrugged. "Gotta have my juice now," he explained. "The restaurant won't serve me any. Damn, I hate being treated like a kid. Especially around my hotshot brother."

In the dark confines of the car, Meredith removed her jacket. Tom eyed her appreciatively. "Now, that's an outfit," he said with approval, drinking some more of the vodka. "I like it. Very grown-up. Very."

Meredith smiled. But inside herself she was having the same doubts she'd been having a lot of lately. She wished Tom would quit drinking. Her chest was starting to feel tight and knotted. Something was very wrong with Tom. Recently she'd been thinking about that a lot.

By the time they arrived at the restaurant where they were meeting Stoney Macreay, Tom had finished half the bottle. "Come on," he said impatiently as he helped Meredith out of the car. "Let's go see the famous brother." His voice was tinged with angry bitterness.

Something more than Tom's drunkenness was wrong. Tom rarely spoke of his home to her, but it didn't take intimate knowledge of his family to realize this double date with Stoney had triggered something bad in Tom's mind.

"Tom," Meredith urged softly, laying a hand on his arm, "we don't have to go here, you know. We can go somewhere else."

"What are you talking about?" he said belligerently. "You think I can't stand up to my big brother? You think I'm ashamed? You think I'm not as good as he is?"

"No, Tom, that's not what I meant at all—"

"Well, come *on,* then."

The restaurant was dark and exclusive and very expensive. When Meredith saw Stoney Macreay and his date—a beautiful, elegant, long-legged blonde—sitting at a far table waiting for them, her heart sank. They looked so... polished, so confident. For a moment she thought she understood exactly how Tom felt. Worriedly she looked at Tom. His handsome face was coldly expressionless, and his hand on her arm was so tight it hurt.

"Here he is," Tom said with forced flippancy when they reached Stoney's table. "The great white hope himself."

Stoney stood politely.

"Meredith Blackmoore," Tom said, draping his arm around Meredith's bare shoulder. "My brother Stoney and..."

"Chrissy Nelson," Stoney supplied. "Hello, Meredith."

His voice was deep and calm. *Kind,* she would think later. Through the years, when she heard that Stoney had said something cutting or grown publicly angry, she would remember when she had first met him, and he had tried to put her at ease. An impossible task.

She had thought that Tom was handsome, but he couldn't come near the male beauty of his older brother. Whatever else the Macreays produced, they created some incredibly good-looking children. Stoney's hair was white blond, his face tanned golden, his eyes thick lashed and colored the hue of a summer storm. Tawny, she named them, with flecks of cinnamon and deep bronze shifting restlessly within.

He was tall, and his charcoal gray blazer made him look almost imperial. He was not as bulky and broad shouldered as his younger brother, but there was something about his ease of movement that reminded her of the fierce grace for which he was famous on the soccer field.

A champion, Meredith thought, holding court with his beautiful lady. And she knew with a certainty she didn't belong here with these incredibly golden people. After all, who was she really? Just a small-town girl with dark hair and pale skin who tried to look grown up by removing the blouse from her jumper.

She was way out of her league.

Well, she would do her best not to make a fool of herself. "Hello," she said gravely, straightening her spine, smiling bravely into Stoney Macreay's eyes. His mouth quirked upward in response, and she had the unmistakable impression that Tom's brother found her somehow amusing. Flushing slightly, she took the chair Tom pulled out for her.

Chrissy smiled at Meredith indulgently. When Stoney sat down, Chrissy placed one of her long, tapered fingers on his arm, the simple gesture one of secure possession. Chrissy's nails glowed crimson in the dull light. "Glad you two could make it," she said to Tom and Meredith. She was wearing a black see-through blouse, through which was visible some extremely lacy black underwear. It was an outfit that was modest and immodest at the same time, and Meredith thought that only a beauty like Chrissy could have pulled it off.

"So what's new, little brother?" Stoney asked, leaning back in his chair. "How's the life?"

"Fantastic!" Tom said grandly. "I set a new record last Thursday...." Made expansive by the alcohol he had consumed, he plunged into a recitation of his sporting accomplishments.

Stoney's lips remained fixed in a resigned upward curve, but Meredith was aware of his expression growing cool. Tom's bragging would have been accepted fine in their usual crowd, but tonight his self-adulation seemed infantile and embarrassing. She glanced up to catch Stoney watching her through eyes that had grown lazy and bored. Once again her face warmed, and she resisted the urge to squirm like a child under his continued regard. As if he sensed her discomfort, Stoney inclined his head to her and winked.

Making a little moue of displeasure, Chrissy placed one of her beautifully manicured hands to a spot high on Stoney Macreay's thigh, and he immediately covered it with his own. Meredith remembered Tom saying that his brother would be having *fun* tonight. She knew what that meant now, and she fought hard to control yet another betraying blush. She knew she was a ninny to react so foolishly. But her sudden sense of isolation was undeniable. She was fast learning that *fun* was the way of the world. Unless she behaved that way herself, she would probably never fit in.

Tom was still rattling on. "Three colleges were there scouting me," he said, his tone taking on an edgy, defensive quality. Meredith was aware that Tom's body language was growing hostile and aggressive. She told herself it was natural for Tom to feel competition with his older brother. Yet she wished he hadn't drunk so much. The more he talked, the angrier he seemed to become. It was as if, in one embarrassingly long, boastful monologue, he had to prove himself equal to Stoney, in honors earned, in games won, in manhood achieved.

Chrissy stifled a yawn, and Tom flushed a bright, furious red. Under the table Meredith saw his hands clench spasmodically. She thought of the vodka he had consumed, and her heart sank. Tom was as close to being as completely out of control as she had ever seen him.

"What about you, Meredith?" Stoney asked when Tom at last fell sullenly silent. "Do you like football?"

"I like to watch Tom play," she offered, hoping to soothe Tom's quickly rising temper. "He's the greatest."

"And...?" he prodded.

"And?" she repeated blankly.

"What else do you like? What are you planning on doing with your life?"

The question startled her. Recently she had done a rather complete job of shelving her own dreams and aspirations. Being Tom's girl had taken all the energy she had.

"I want to be a doctor," she said slowly. "That's what my dad is."

"A doctor!" Tom started to laugh uproariously. "Why in hell do you need to be anything? You stick around me, and you'll never have to do anything except paint your pretty little toenails. I'm going to be famous, famous as my big brother here. Hell, even more famous—"

"Tom," Stoney interrupted coldly. "That's *enough.*"

"*What?*"

"You're drunk, Tom. You're making a fool of yourself and you're humiliating your girl—"

"The hell you say—" Tom half rose from his chair.

"I say."

"I'm not drunk! Ask Meredith. She'll tell you! Am I drunk, sweet Merry? Am I? Tell old Stoney the truth."

"He's..." Meredith began before falling helplessly silent.

"What are you doing, Tom?" Stoney's voice was cold sober and rock hard. "You're in training. It's the middle of the season. What are you trying to do, follow in the old man's footsteps? How will you accomplish anything if you don't even have the discipline to—"

"What about you, big brother?" Tom interrupted sarcastically. "What's that in your glass?" He laughed mockingly. "It sure isn't milk!"

Stoney shook his head in disgust. "I'm in training, too, Tom." He lifted his glass. "Apple juice."

"Well, la-di-da," Tom said, still standing. "Excuse me. I forgot I was dining with some sort of lily-white hero. You think you're better 'n me, don't you, Stoney? Hell, you think you're better than half this whole crazy world. Don't you? *Don't you?*"

Stoney sat, his lion's eyes darkening, his face inscrutable. He said nothing.

"Stoney, honey," Chrissy said, once again placing her hand on his arm. "We're all finished eating. Weren't we going to go dancing?"

Stoney took his time answering. He seemed to be engaged in some internal struggle. At last he turned to his date. Meredith watched as a slow, glamorous smile formed itself on his face. She wondered if she were the only one that noticed that the smile didn't reach his eyes—that those intelligent, tawny orbs remained aloof and distant. "Sorry, darling," he said. "Of course we'll go and dance." He leaned over and kissed Chrissy lightly on her lips.

Meredith, watching them, felt her stomach do a strange little flip-flop. Beside her, Tom snorted angrily.

Stoney helped Chrissy to her feet. "We'll all go in my car," he said flatly.

"What's the matter?" Tom said, leaning half over the table. "You think I can't drive? I can drive fine. Besides, Meredith has to be in by the stroke of midnight. I'll need my car to take the little innocent Cinderella home." Tom sounded rude and taunting. He put his hand heavily on Meredith's bare shoulder.

All eyes turned her way, and Meredith wished she could sink right through the floor. She remembered her friend Joy enviously describing her as a fairy-tale princess, and gave a brave smile. She didn't understand the animosity between Tom and his brother, but the tension it created was stronger than anything Meredith had felt within her own family. She hardly knew how to react.

"My parents care about me," she said at last. "I'm not even sixteen yet. That's why I have to go home."

"Sure," Tom said. "Home to Mommy and Daddy, who'll probably never let you grow up—"

Abruptly Meredith shoved her chair back and stood. "Actually," she said, not looking at anybody, "I think I'd rather go home right now, Tom. I'm feeling awfully tired—"

Tom's eyes narrowed to slits. He put his arm around her waist and pulled her close. "Meredith," he said with exaggerated patience, but it was easy for Meredith to hear the underlying threat in his voice. "You know you love to dance. Come along, just for a little while, honey. I promise I'll get you safely home on time."

It was then, in that moment, that Meredith realized the pretense was over. She didn't care for Tom Macreay at all. Not a bit. She might be young, but she knew with absolute certainty that she didn't need this, not for any kind of popularity or status. That he should bring her here, drunk, and badger her in front of his brother and his brother's date was unforgivable. She wanted to go home. She raised her head to tell him so.

But the words died in her throat as she looked into Tom's face. His expression was dark and ugly, and she realized that his arm held so punishingly tight around her waist was trembling slightly.

He was ready to explode. If she crossed him now, who knew what kind of scene he would make? The evening was bad enough already.

The night couldn't last forever, she reasoned. She would go dancing with Tom and then go home, and she would never accept a date with him again.

"All right," she said slowly. "But don't make fun of my family again, Tom."

"Of course not, babe." Tom laughed. "Why would I do that?"

Stoney looked at Meredith. His eyes were hard. "Are you sure?" he said.

"Of course she's sure," Tom said, squeezing Meredith against his football-trained body.

"That's a beautiful young lady you've got. Treat her right, Tom," Stoney ordered softly.

"Absolutely, big brother. You bet," Tom said. Then he added, almost slyly, "We'll meet you at the club. I have something...private...to say to Meredith, so we might not be there right away."

"Tom—" Stoney put his hand on his brother's shoulder.

Tom jerked away. "We'll be *along*," he practically snarled. "See you there."

Meredith closed her eyes. It'll be over, she reassured herself. Soon.

Her sixteenth birthday was next week. It would be years before she would remember that and be able to forgive herself her impressionable youth and innocence. Tom didn't drive her directly to the club. Instead, he drove to a forested area where he proceeded to force himself on her then acted as if he had done nothing wrong.

The fact that she'd been raped would be a long time sinking in—after all, she didn't really fight, didn't scream, didn't even tell Tom afterward how much she'd hated it. She just sat there and listened to Tom tell her that she was a woman now, and then, her body burning and her mind withdrawn, she went dancing with him.

But the vodka finally sent him over the edge. By the time he led her onto the dance floor, he was weaving from drunkenness.

She was grateful that the dance club was dimly lit and full—and that the live band was so loud. She didn't have to think in this press, didn't have to feel. If only Tom could stay upright, she'd be all right.

Stoney and Chrissy were dancing when they came in. Out of the corner of her eye, Meredith saw Stoney frown sharply and say something to his date before seating her at a table. Then he came across the dance floor to where she and Tom were attempting to move, and cut in.

"Wha ya want?" Tom slurred.

"Sit down," Stoney said through gritted teeth. *"Now."*

For once Tom didn't argue. Looking sick, he stumbled off in the direction of the men's room.

Meredith found herself dancing with Stoney Macreay.

It was strange really. Just a few hours before, she would have been in a daze of disbelief and happiness to be partnered by such a hero; surely she would be the envy of every girl at Colton High. Yet all she felt now was stiff and numb, fragmented.

"Are you all right?" Stoney asked. The band was playing an especially schmaltzy version of "We've Only Just Begun," and Meredith locked a frantic bit of choked laughter in her throat. Stoney was a much better dancer than his brother, she thought with distant clarity. Just as she had suspected, his was a totally natural grace.

"Meredith." He gave her a little shake.

"What? Oh. Fine."

"Did you and Tom fight?"

"No." Something had happened to her normal reactions; she had the oddest desire to bury her head in Stoney's shoulder and sleep.

"Nothing happened on the way here? You guys took a long time."

Her natural honesty asserted itself; she couldn't tell such a big lie. "Why the third degree?" she asked instead, but even to her own ears her flippancy sounded desperate. "Are you your brother's keeper or something?"

"Something happened," Stoney said flatly. "You look . . . shattered."

No, she wasn't, she thought fiercely. "I'm *dandy,*" she said. Yet she knew she was holding herself together by a fine, brittle thread. There was no way she was going to allow that thread to break—she would splinter apart then, and how would she ever put herself back together? Momentarily she closed her eyes.

But Stoney wouldn't let her alone. "Is he often like this?"

"Yes." Her tone was bitter.

"Why do you go out with him, then?"

"Because he's the school hero," she answered curtly, for a brief second allowing her newly acquired self-loathing to show. "Like *you,* Stoney. An all-American hero." The laugh she had tried hard to control came out in a strained hiccup, and she realized that her breaking point was dangerously near. "Dumb jock hero," she muttered.

"Yeah," he agreed grimly. "And you're not a dumb girl, Meredith." The music ended. "I'll take you home," he said.

She wasn't about to argue. "All right," she whispered. "Please."

Stoney walked her over to Chrissy's table. "I'm taking Meredith home. Do you want to come, or shall I put you in a taxi?"

Chrissy's perfectly made-up lips turned down. "Aren't you a little old to be playing nursemaid, Stoney, honey?"

she asked. "You can't rescue every waif that Tom picks up."

Meredith stared at Chrissy miserably. "She's right. I should be the one taking the taxi," she offered. "If you'll just help me—"

"No," Stoney said. Then, in a gesture that seemed curiously calculated, he put his hand around Chrissy's neck and whispered something in her ear.

Feeling more alone than ever, Meredith looked away.

The blonde relaxed, stretched a little and smiled. "All right, darling," she said pleasurably. "I'll be waiting."

"Do that." His hand stroked Chrissy's long white throat.

A few minutes later Stoney handed Meredith into his sports car. It was a black-and-white model, its lines sleek and smooth, its interior as comfortable as a down pillow. She arranged herself in the passenger seat and stared out the window.

Stoney studied her in silence. Then he said quietly, "Where to, Miss Blackmoore?"

Except for Meredith's soft, expressionless voice giving Stoney directions, they drove the entire way in silence. From time to time she sensed Stoney's eyes looking her way, but she refused to acknowledge his glances—she kept her head turned as she stared bleakly out at the night landscape.

When Stoney turned up her broad circular driveway, his headlights illuminated her parent's large two-story brick home. Her mother's semiformal layout of flowers and blossoming shrubs decorated the front yard; just visible in the back was the swimming pool that her father had installed last year. "Tom must love this," he murmured sardonically.

"Excuse me?"

Stoney slid a look her way. "Have you ever been to our house, Meredith?"

"No. Why?"

Stoney shrugged. "It's not like this," he said obliquely. "I begin to see the attraction."

He was talking in riddles, and Meredith was too numb to care. She put her hand on the door handle. "Thanks for bringing me home," she said politely.

"Wait," Stoney said.

She looked at him resentfully. Her face felt stiff, like thin paper. She wasn't going to be able to hold up much longer.

"You've got magnificent eyes," Stoney said. "All dark and mysterious. Beautiful. Only right now they look frightened, like some wild thing that's been wounded in the night. What did my brother do to you, Meredith?"

"He didn't do *anything*," she said fiercely, in that moment needing more than life itself to deny what had happened to her. When she saw stark disbelief in Stoney's face, she added harshly, "Nothing important anyway. He was just being a jerk, Stoney."

Stoney took her chin in his hand and turned her to face him. "You're a lovely child, Meredith Blackmoore."

"Don't *touch* me," she ordered in sudden violent reaction.

"But you're not for Tom," he said, not letting her go. "I hope to God you're not sleeping with him."

She flushed bright red, and the eyes he had just praised filled with hot, willful tears. She couldn't have been more obvious had she shouted the truth aloud. Stoney's face darkened in angry comprehension.

"Let *go* of me," she said, dashing the tears away. "I'm not your business."

"Dammit!" Stoney exploded. "What do you two think you're doing? Are you at least being *careful?* Have the two of you even *thought* about that?"

"Tom doesn't *think* about anything," she replied furiously. "And you misunderstand. I'm not *sleeping* with your brother. After tonight I'm not even dating him anymore."

"Good," Stoney said grimly. "A wise decision, Meredith. Keep studying and go to college and become a doctor, just like you said. Don't let my brother mess things up for you."

"I won't," she whispered, feeling her eyes grow hot again. From somewhere deep inside herself, she felt a fierce determination begin to burn. Nothing was going to change for her because of tonight. *Nothing.*

She met Stoney's hard gaze. "What about *your* date? Chrissy?" Her voice was cool. "Are you messing up *her* life?"

He stared at her. "She knows the score."

"Oh. I see. The score. How silly of me. Of course."

"Meredith—"

"Thanks for the advice," she said.

His hand reached out to rub her cheek, and this time she didn't flinch away. He smiled coldly. "Not that I blame my brother," he said slowly. "You're exquisite. If you were a little older, I'd be interested myself—"

"Leave me alone," she snapped. "I'm not your type."

Stoney turned from her to take a long deliberate look at her parents' large, well-tended, prosperous home. "You're right about that, Meredith Blackmoore," he said, and there was some hidden anger in him, some darkness, that had her looking at him once more.

They sat for a moment, staring at each other. Then he said roughly, "You really are a baby." He added, "But tonight when you go to sleep, remember this last word of wisdom from Stoney Macreay. Stay in your own bed, little girl, and stay out of my brother's. Stay out of anybody's."

But Stoney's advice had come too late, and was thus no longer needed. She was already determined to never *ever* let anybody do to her again what Tom Macreay had done. Even if it meant sleeping alone for the rest of her life.

Chapter Three

Everything did change for Meredith, though. Nothing remained the same. Not her plans for college, not the rest of her high school life, not even her friends.

And Tess had been the biggest change of all....

When Meredith was still in her first trimester, her mother and father insisted the three of them visit Tom's family. Her father called Mr. Macreay on the phone and arranged an evening for all of them to meet.

As they drove to Tom's house, Meredith began to get an inkling of what Stoney had meant the night he took her home. The Macreay house was at the end of a long, rutted two-track lane, about ten miles outside of town. The house itself was small and cheaply built, and appeared even more desolate by its lack of care: deep holes in the driveway and shutters hanging crazily from the windows, old blue paint peeling from the siding, a screen torn jaggedly and half pulled out of the door. To the left, a satellite dish rose in surrealistic splendor above a yard full of dog droppings and broken toys.

The woman who answered their knock had a gray pinched face, and was wearing a faded housedress. "I'm SueLynn," she offered with a flat, lifeless smile. "Please come in."

They followed her through a short hall to the living room. The furniture there was old and soiled; the sofa had a hole gouged in one arm. But, at odds with the outside of the house, the room *was* tidy. And in the corner opposite the door was a truly beautiful chair—a fine old oak piece with a needlepoint design of multicolored flowers sewn onto the seat. On the coffee table was a canning jar filled with dried wildflowers.

Tom and his dad were already there, waiting for them. Meredith had met Asa Macreay several times, at Tom's games. He was a big man with a bloated face and small, squinty eyes. He was seated on the sofa; Tom was using an overstuffed easy chair, across from his father.

They were both nursing beers, watching television.

"Asa," SueLynn said timidly. "The Blackmoores are here."

"Well. So I see. Sit down," Asa said, smiling grandly. "Make yourself at home." Then he added, "Tom, turn off the TV, boy."

Tom used a remote to shut the television down. He didn't look at Meredith and slouched down in his chair.

"Hudson. And Kathleen, isn't it?" Asa asked, speaking to her parents. "What's up?"

Meredith's mother had gone immediately to the oak chair. "Why, what a lovely piece," she said with genuine warmth. "Did you refinish this, SueLynn?"

SueLynn's expression brightened. "Yes," she said. "Stoney found it for me at an auction, and he brought it here for me to work on."

"You did the needlepoint, too?" Kathleen Blackmoore asked.

SueLynn, straightening a little, nodded.

"It's truly beautiful work."

Asa laughed, and the light that had begun to appear in SueLynn's eyes dimmed. "Now, I'm sure you didn't come here to admire the decorating," he said, his words slurring noticeably. He inclined his head. "What's up, Hudson?"

Meredith's dad looked first at Tom's father, then at SueLynn. Her father never was one for beating around the bush, so Meredith was unsurprised when he said, simply, "Asa. SueLynn. It appears that Meredith is pregnant with Tom's child."

Silence reigned. Asa looked at Meredith, his beer-glazed eyes moving to her still flat stomach. SueLynn's already white face paled further. Finally Asa raised his can to his lips and took a deep swallow before turning to stare coldly at his son. "The hell you say." Tom's face had flushed beet red.

This was worse than anything she could have expected. Meredith wished the floor would open up and swallow her whole.

Before anyone could respond to Asa's comment, the sounds of a childish fight erupted in another part of the house, and a girl started to wail. "Mommy! Mooommy!" Then the crying child was at the living-room door, running to bury her head against SueLynn's stomach.

"Billy hit me! Hard! It hurt!"

SueLynn patted the girl's head. "Go *away*, Clarissa," she said, her soft voice sounding thin and desperate.

"But, Mommy—"

"Get out of here, brat." Tom's first words of the evening were spoken in a low snarl.

"Please, Mommy—"

Suddenly Asa Macreay rose from the sofa, his face twisted in threatening anger. He made a fist with his right hand. "You heard your mother!" His rage was sudden and powerful; Meredith could feel Clarissa's fear. "Get *out*," Asa said.

Clarissa's face turned pasty white. "Mommy—" she whispered.

"*Out!*" Asa roared, taking a step toward the child, his fist raised in striking position.

The child fled.

Asa turned a smug face to Hudson Blackmoore. *That,* he seemed to be saying, *is how I handle my problems.* Meredith watched in amazed horror as the remnants of his sudden fury died from his beady eyes, to be replaced by a look that could only be described as crafty.

"Now, then," he said to Hudson. "Your girl's knocked up, eh? And she's trying to pin the blame on *my* boy?"

"She's pregnant. And the father is Tom," Meredith's dad said quietly.

"How does she know?" Asa sneered.

Meredith saw her mother, still standing by the chair in the corner, stiffen in outrage.

"What did you say?" She had never heard her father use that tone of voice before, to anyone. Though he wasn't speaking loudly, her father sounded almost...dangerous.

Asa shrugged insolently. "You ever touch this girl, Tom?" he said.

Tom looked at Meredith. She stared back helplessly. He glanced uneasily at his father. He shifted his attention back to his beer.

"I'm waiting for an answer, boy."

"Never," Tom said at last in a low voice, speaking into the can. "If she's got a brat in her belly, it's not mine."

Disbelief washed through Meredith. It had never occurred to her that Tom would deny his role in what had happened. "It's *yours*," she blurted. "That night we went out with Stoney—"

"Nothing happened that night," Tom said, still not meeting her eyes. "We went out to eat. Dancing. I took you home."

"But—" Meredith said.

"See?" Asa growled. "Your daughter's filled little oven could be just about anybody's, couldn't it? *Except* my Tom's."

"Asa, these are the *Blackmoores* you're talking to," SueLynn hissed.

"Shut up," Asa snapped.

Meredith's mother left the corner to stand by her husband. "Meredith doesn't lie," she said.

Hudson looked long and hard at Tom, still seated in the overstuffed chair. "You know the truth," he spoke with deadly quiet. "And you know what's right, young man."

Again Tom's face colored. He opened his mouth to speak, then closed it. He looked again at Meredith, and stumbled to his feet. "Actually—"

But before he could utter another word, Asa gave him a rough shove back into the chair. "He's going to do what's right, all right." Asa's face was swollen with anger. "He's going to have nothing more to do with the little tramp you've brought into my house. He's got a big football scholarship, and my Tom is good enough to go pro. He's going to be a hero. Just like his big brother, Stoney. Isn't that right, Tom? He's going to turn out just like Stoney. Nothing like your little girl there is going to trap him and get in the way of his future."

Meredith's father was a tall man, and in good shape. For a moment he stood silent, his hands fisted, his mouth grim, the pulse in his neck beating wildly. Meredith had never seen him like this. Her breath caught in her throat. Pride filled her that he wasn't like Asa Macreay. Then the shame came, for what she had done, for somehow being the cause of this terrible scene. It occurred to her that it didn't really matter whether Tom ever acknowledged what he had done. The truth was, she'd like to forget it, herself. "Please, Daddy," she spoke before anything else could happen. "Let's just go home."

Kathleen Blackmoore reached for her husband's hand. "An excellent suggestion," she said, her own rage evident in her steely control. "We will accomplish nothing here."

"Yeah!" Asa was shouting now. "Get out! This is my house." He thumped himself on his chest. "You have no call to come here— to *my* house—insulting *my* boy!"

"We're leaving," Meredith's father said frigidly. With a jerk of his head, he directed Meredith and her mom out of the Macreay home.

Before they reached the front door, they heard a splintering crash.

"My chair!" they heard SueLynn cry out, just once.

"Damned thing anyway." Asa was obviously in a fury. "Gave you airs. Couldn't even sit on it without you worrying about it." Then he said, "Well, what are you waiting for, woman? Clean it up! And bring me some more beer."

Meredith walked in stunned silence with her parents to their car. She remembered Stoney Macreay looking at her parents' home and warning her away from his brother.

As they drove away, her father said, "I'll call my lawyer tomorrow. We'll make sure they never get any paternal rights, ever."

Her mother nodded before speaking directly to Meredith. "It's all right, baby. We're here for you. We'll help you."

Baby. Stoney had called her that, too. But she was *pregnant* now. She *couldn't* be a baby anymore. She had someone else to live for now. Someone else for whom she was responsible. It was time she grew up, fast.

Late in her pregnancy she went grocery shopping for her mother. Her added bulk made her clumsy; she dropped a can of pineapple she had pulled off the shelves. As she bent to pick it up, she felt a sharp pain in her abdomen and gasped slightly, holding her swollen belly until the pain passed. Then she reached awkwardly for the can.

Only there was a male hand there before her, reaching for the tinned pineapple. As she slowly straightened, she found herself looking into the inscrutable tawny eyes of Stoney Macreay.

He was wearing casual jeans and a golden sweater. His hair was slightly longer than when they'd met; it curled around his neck. A single blond lock fell down onto his forehead. He looked as regal as ever, as out of place in that small-town grocery as the Prince of Wales would have looked riding a London trolley. Even after everything that had happened, Tom's brother still had the power to awe her.

Stoney's gaze traveled from her face to the swelling of her body. She fastened her hands around the grocery-cart handle and faced him with shaky defiance.

"Is that my brother's work?" he asked abruptly.

"He says it's not."

"So I heard."

That rattled her. "Tom told you?" she asked in disbelief.

"No," he said steadily, watching her eyes. "I got that gem of information from my mother. She told me you came to our house."

She didn't want to think about that. "Yes."

Stoney gave a small, grave nod. His expression was oddly gentle, almost apologetic. "That must have been an experience."

Color tinged her cheeks slightly.

"Certainly nothing like you've been used to, Miss Blackmoore."

She looked away. She didn't know what to say. She couldn't imagine what it would have been like, growing up in a house like that.

Stoney's mouth narrowed in wry comprehension; his eyes grew distant. "I've tried to help them, you know." He made a shrugging motion. "But my dad—he sort of uses everything up."

He sounded as though he was talking about the weather. Only the little white lines around his mouth gave him away, and his lion's eyes that suddenly seemed colder than a winter storm spoke of some inner tension. She felt a surge of compassion. Yet he was, after all, still Stoney Macreay. Way out of her league. "You don't have to justify your father to me," she blurted. "He's not your fault."

"Such wisdom," he murmured, his eyes refocusing on her face. "Too bad you weren't wise about...some other things."

His too accurate words were coolly spoken, making her feel more awkward than ever. Face reality, she told herself. Stoney Macreay didn't need her sympathy. No matter what he'd come from, he'd done all right. He had everything he wanted. Which was more than she could say about herself. "You don't know anything," Meredith retorted sharply. She held out her hand. "May I have my pineapple, Stoney?"

"What about you, young Meredith? Are you still in school?"

"Yes."

"Well," Stoney said. "That's good."

Meredith felt something in her start to give. Right, she thought. Good. Fine. Ha. Nothing could be further from the truth. She didn't know why Stoney Macreay was even talking to her. It wasn't as if she was his problem or anything. And he certainly didn't need anybody feeling sorry for him, as she almost had just a minute ago—he was probably the most self-sufficient person she'd ever met. She decided she just wanted her can of pineapple, so she could finish her shopping and go home. "Everything's great, Stoney," she said brittlely. "Peachy." She thought of the alternative school she was attending—the one for kids with special problems. It didn't matter there that her young body was swelling with new life; there were students at the alternative school with a lot worse problems than hers.

His eyes darkened at her tone. "I told you you weren't for him." He sounded sternly remote.

"You were too late." Pineapple or not, she was going to leave him. Her mother would have to use a different recipe. She started to turn away.

"Meredith." Unexpectedly he cupped his hand around her cheek, effectively keeping her from moving farther. "Look, if you ever need anything—"

Then he stopped talking. His thumb moved slowly down the line of her jaw. She stared at him, disoriented, barely breathing, while he hovered over her. Confusion swam with other feelings inside her very pregnant body. Stoney, she saw, looked stunned.

He dropped his hand and backed away. "If you ever need anything—" this time his tone was flat and totally expressionless "—call me."

She shook her head and, still bemused, spoke unthinkingly. "This baby is nothing to you, Stoney. You're a Macreay. We're... my father is working with our lawyer to ensure... My father says I'm to have absolutely no contact with the Macreay family. I shouldn't even be talking to you."

His golden eyes flared slightly. But all he said was, "I see."

"Now, may I please have the pineapple?"

He handed it to her, his movements slow and deliberate. Yet she couldn't help but be aware of a coiled strength there, beneath the steely control. She imagined him moving across a soccer field.

She reached out to take the can of fruit. But he didn't let go. Instead, he wrapped his other hand around hers, so that both of them were holding the can now, her hand encircled by both of his. He said very quietly, "You picked the wrong brother, Meredith Blackmoore. I wouldn't give my baby up. Not for anything."

"Well," she said, looking anywhere but at him, "it's not yours."

"I'm its uncle, though, aren't I? I don't know about the rest of my dysfunctional family, but I'd like to keep in touch, Meredith."

Then his hand tightened almost imperceptibly, and she again was lost, feeling strangely warm and confused. But she had to do what was right, what her father said she should do. "After the papers are filed, you won't be anything, Stoney. This baby will have no relation to any Macreay at all. Ever." She couldn't believe how bereft and sad she sounded.

At her words he went all bleak and still, his tawny lion's eyes burning some message that in her confusion she failed to understand. "Damn Tom," he said savagely. "Damn you for thinking a little piece of paper can take away what I am. I'll be an uncle, all right."

Again she shook her head, harder. His anger strengthened her, buoyed her up. "No. You won't. Not legally anyway. You may be a big star, Stoney. You may be used to getting your way. But don't—don't fool with me. Don't try to belong to my child. What I'm doing is hard enough—I don't need to be messed up by another Macreay hero."

With firm determination, she turned to leave him, but before she could take a first step, his hand was on her shoulder, turning her back to him. "I learned a long time ago never to listen to nevers, Meredith." His laugh was harsh and hard. "If I *fooled* with you, it would only be because you wanted me to." She breathed in sharply, staring at him big eyed as he continued, soft and dangerous, "And it wouldn't kill your child to know it had an uncle named Stoney Macreay."

"My father says—"

"And don't you ever confuse me with my brother—"

"—I'll be protected by law."

He scared her, he looked so mad. So furiously golden. Something's going on here, she thought, that has nothing to do with me. But he scared her just the same.

Then he seemed to soften, and he shook his head ruefully. "Damn," he said. "Look, Meredith. I'm sorry. Don't look so...ah... But you can't help it, can you? So damned exquisite even when you're scared. Look. I just want to keep in touch, that's all. Nothing more. Kind of watch over my nephew. Or niece. Whatever."

"You can't," she repeated stupidly. "My father—"

Again his eyes blazed at her, flaming bright and hard and somehow mocking. It was all she could do not to take a step backward. Then he looked away. For the first time Meredith noticed that they had collected a small audience—local people who were working hard at pretending they weren't listening, studying the rows of food with carefully blank expressions. Her face flamed.

"All right," Stoney said at last, speaking the words as if forcing himself to be calm. "I understand. Everything's wrapped up, nice and tight and legal. Which is no more than Tom deserves, not that he cares much. But I care. And I'll be around, Meredith Blackmoore. If you ever need anything, don't forget what I said."

She shook her head blindly and pushed the cart to the checkout counter. The whole encounter had shaken her badly. Remembering what Stoney had said about pick-

ing the wrong brother, she felt strangely like crying.
Which was really stupid, because she was sure that never
again in her whole life would she ever *ever* want anything from another jock hero. Especially not Tom's famous older brother, no matter how much of a big shot he
was.

And Stoney hadn't been around. Not really. He'd been
too busy playing soccer. Playing the crowds. Playing the
women. But she knew he never forgot.

When Meredith delivered Tess, a small bouquet of
daisies had been sent anonymously and placed among the
flowers and gifts that Meredith had received from family and friends. And later, each year on Tess's birthday,
the child received a present from an unknown "secret
pal." The gifts were never too large or too expensive, just
small tasteful reminders that someone out there was
keeping track of the passing years in Tess's life.

Still, before he came home to Colton, Meredith only
saw Stoney one more time, and that was a freak occur-
rence—one of those rare circumstances that should never
have happened but sometimes do. When she was nine-
teen, Meredith and two-year-old Tess had accompanied
Meredith's mother on a shopping trip to Chicago. The
day was warm and breezy, and Meredith had tied her
dark hair back in a careless ponytail. They were walking
down Michigan Avenue, little Tess in a stroller, getting
ready to turn into Marshall Field's, when she felt the unmistakable prickle on her neck that told her she was being watched. Turning, she saw Stoney Macreay standing
not ten feet away, looking at her. With him were two
other men. They were laughing easily, as if someone had
just made a joke. Then, noticing their friend's preoccupation, the two men fell silent and looked to see what had
caught Stoney's attention.

Meredith stood perfectly still, her chin up, her back straight. She watched as his eyes traveled to Tess, how something in him seemed to soften and grow angry all at once. He disengaged himself from his group at the same time that she turned from him, preparing to follow her mother into the store.

His hand reached her arm just before she opened the door. "Meredith Blackmoore," he said quietly.

She stopped. "Stoney," she managed to say coolly, not looking at him. "What are you doing in Chicago?"

"How wonderful to know you're keeping up with my career," he said dryly. "I've a big match tomorrow, Meredith. World Cup."

"Oh." She gave him a bright smile. "Good luck."

She would have left him then, except he reached out and with a tug pulled the stroller backward, out of her reach. Without so much as asking her permission, he lowered his tall frame down to kneel beside it and looked at Tess. Meredith's daughter was worn out from shopping and was sleeping peacefully.

Tess was a lovely child. She had Meredith's dark hair and eyes, and her skin was porcelain clear.

"So. Here she is," Stoney said softly. "A pretty thing." He looked around at Meredith. "Is she happy?"

"Yes," Meredith answered curtly. "I've got to go, Stoney."

"She looks content." His hand surrounded Tess's dark head. Stayed. Tess shifted in her seat, leaning her small cheek into Stoney's hand.

Meredith's breath caught in her throat. "Stoney—"

"Yeah. I know. She doesn't even know who I am." He stood up in the lazy way she remembered. "You going to be around tomorrow?" he asked almost carelessly.

It took her a fraction of a second to realize that he was actually feeling her out to see if she wanted to come to his game.

As if she would be interested. As if any macho man running around on a field of sport would hold any interest for her whatsoever.

Yet for one wild and crazy moment, she was actually tempted. There was no rational reason for it, no logic. But the desire was there just the same.

She gave herself an inward shake. "No," she said firmly. "We're leaving in the morning."

"Too bad. I could've gotten you tickets."

"Thanks anyway," she said.

He smiled somewhat grimly. "I haven't forgotten you, Meredith Blackmoore. Or your daughter."

She stared at him, thinking of the small stuffed horse that had come by UPS four months ago, on Tess's birthday. "I have to go," she said.

He nodded then, his fingers touching her cheek lightly in a mock salute. "Sure," he said. "But first—" Then he bent his head and touched his lips to hers.

It was a light, fleeting caress. The briefest possible jolt of pure sensuality. She told herself later it signified nothing. Stoney Macreay gave his kisses to lots of women, after all.

It was just that she hadn't been kissed in a very long time.

She met his gaze, stunned. He smiled crookedly. "So long," he said.

She watched him rejoin his friends before she turned and pushed the baby carriage into the department store, in search of her own mother.

That was the last time she'd seen Stoney before he came to Colton, even though Tess's presents had kept coming, year after year. And since he'd been in Colton, he'd not sought her out. It was Meredith who had forced the meeting by coming to Roger's game.

But now that she had, she was aware of a tension coiling deep inside her, some latent, intuitive knowledge that she had played into his hands, that he had been waiting for her to make the first move.

She hadn't meant to. It was just that her parents were right—she couldn't stay away from all of Roger's games or avoid Stoney Macreay forever.

Only her parents thought her reticence came from some lingering hostility toward anything and anyone Macreay.

They were only partly right.

The other part involved her own secret fear that Stoney had come home to Colton specifically because she and Tess were still here.

Stoney Macreay was a man whose life had revolved around games, she told herself firmly. Somehow she would have to make him understand that this game was one he couldn't win—that neither she nor Tess was his to play with.

Stop being silly, she instructed herself. She was six years older and decades wiser than she'd been when she'd first met him. Surely only a foolish child could maintain the pretense that Stoney had come to Colton to chase someone like herself.

And besides, he had his blonde. He obviously wasn't interested in Meredith.

Which made her feel worse than ever, because if she *was* so old and wise and unavailable, why had she then been so short and defensive with Stoney, who only wanted to talk with the child they both knew was his niece? His curiosity about Tess was surely normal.

Because he made her afraid, that's why. Because if Stoney hadn't come to Colton because of Tess and her, then what other reason was there? His family wasn't here. As far as she knew, he had no close friends here. And she doubted he'd come for a team of high school soccer players—he could coach anywhere.

No, the only people who might be remotely important to Stoney were herself and her daughter.

She'd grown a lot, but she'd tucked certain emotions carefully away. Seeing Stoney today had made her remember things she hadn't allowed herself to think about in a very long time. And the memories had stirred feelings that weren't buried so deep after all—so that suddenly she was filled with a yearning vulnerability so intense it frightened her.

Which was, she told herself, reason enough to continue to stay away from Stoney Macreay.

Chapter Four

Stoney Macreay thought about Meredith Blackmoore all the way home: the way she'd gone all still when he'd first seen her, high up on the bleachers, with the wind blowing her hair. The coolness in her dark eyes when he'd approached her in the park. The way she'd been with her small, bright-eyed daughter, possessive and proud.

He pulled into his driveway, killed the engine and sat bemused and silent. Karen was still sitting next to him, her hand still on his leg. He knew his preoccupation was unforgivably rude. Yet he seemed unable to control it, just as he'd been unable to control so many things lately. All he could do was see Meredith's incredibly beautiful brown eyes, so expressively hostile. He wondered how her eyes would look when she was soft and yielding. The thought pierced him, and he caught his breath in sudden yearning.

"Stoney," Karen said at last, her tone carefully neutral. "Quit brooding. Look at me."

Distractedly obedient, he looked. A wry half smile curved his lips. Here was a good-looking, available woman sitting right next to him. *Her* eyes weren't giving any hands-off signals. Her mouth curved upward in a provocative, coaxing curve. Her body leaned willingly forward. "Come on," she said huskily. "Show me your house."

He tried to will Meredith's image out of his brain and almost succeeded. He got out of his car and walked around to open Karen's door. She got out slowly, deliberately, in one long, fluid, sinuous movement, showing him just a hint of cleavage, letting him get a good look at legs encased in skintight jeans.

When they were inside his house, Karen turned to him. She put her arms around his neck, moved close against his chest, pulled his head down, opened her mouth against his and whispered, "Kiss me, darling."

God, he felt so empty.

He hadn't seen Karen in over two months, had never dated her steadily or exclusively. Yet here he was, alone in his house with her, and she, too, obviously had one thing in mind.

Yet he'd been happy enough to see her this afternoon. Before he'd known Meredith was there. He'd known she'd been avoiding him, and that knowledge hurt. For a brief moment it had been sweet, soothing balm to know that a woman like Karen would come chasing him all the way to a small town like Colton.

Just like the old days, when he could have any woman he wanted.

Almost.

Again a picture of Meredith's face formed in his brain. She'd looked at him so very coolly, so distantly. *She* hadn't wanted to kiss him. *She* hadn't wanted him around at all.

Hell, he thought in self-disgust. He looked at Karen with growing discomfort. This obviously wasn't going to work. He put his hands on Karen's shoulders and waited.

She continued to move against him, her face turned up to his, her eyes closed expectantly. "Baby," she said, rubbing both her hands over his back. "Darling." She nuzzled his neck and raised a leg to brush his.

"Karen."

She looked up into his face with eyes that had gone moist with lascivious heat. Her entire face seemed covered with a sheen of lustful, unconfined concupiscence. "Stoney," she said, making his name sound like that of some carnal, unchaste god.

Was he supposed to be flattered? he thought wearily. Yet the harsh voice of honesty reminded him of times that he was.

He lifted an eyebrow and said to her, almost quizzically, "I'm starving. I want to eat."

He watched as a variety of expressions flitted across Karen's openly sensual face. Confusion first. Then disbelief. Then stunned anger. And something else, barely caught before she lowered her lashes against his steady gaze—something vulnerable and frightened and very alone.

"What?" she said.

"I haven't eaten since breakfast," he told her, his words coming out more gently than he had consciously intended.

She took a small step away from him. She looked at him again, her eyes almost blank, her body, he thought, almost under control.

"You want to eat now?" she said.

"Yeah. I'll take you out to dinner," he offered.

"Sure, honey," Karen said, tossing her head, trying to hide her disappointment. "We can always come back here later."

He let the comment go unanswered as he hustled her out his door. But he knew there wasn't going to be a later. Not with Karen, anyway.

The clean Colton air swept through his lungs, and he breathed in deeply. "Ah," he said. "Beautiful day, don't you think?"

He took Karen to the most expensive restaurant Colton had. It was going to be the best he could do in the way of apology, he admitted to himself, though for the life of him he couldn't say exactly what he was apologizing for.

For not performing on demand, perhaps. For not being anymore what he'd been in the past.

For not giving her a ride from the great Stoney Macreay.

The dinner was not a success.

On the way to the restaurant, Karen opened her blouse just enough so that he could see the black filmy lace she was wearing underneath. Her skin was white and lush, her cleavage deep. She ate her food with dainty sensuality, restrained now, subdued. Halfway through the meal, her lips were still wet and glossy from the lipstick she was wearing—he found himself wondering how she managed that trick. He knew she hadn't given up—her eyes, made up to sultry perfection, continued to meet his with open desire.

I'm getting old, Stoney thought. Much too old and tired to play this game.

Meredith would never come on to a man like this, he thought. It wouldn't be her style. He remembered how she looked, sitting on those small-town bleachers with her hair all loose and flying around her shoulders, her face scrubbed clean, her arm around the little girl who looked so delightfully happy—not tense and afraid and shy like some faces he had known. He'd wanted to stare at the child forever, until his heart memorized the innocence and pleasure in that little face, so that somehow he could really know that children could look like that.

His niece. Though she'd never be told that fact, he supposed.

Tess. He tested the name in his mind. An easy name to remember, to like. Just like the child, with eyes as dark as her mother's, smiling up at him with such cheerful trust.

He remembered his sisters, growing up in his father's house. Closed little faces, filled with fear. Skinny, underfed bodies, always hiding from their father's voice and hand. And his mother, looking pinched and defeated and old before her time, enduring with silent stoicism the utterly unendurable.

Tess wouldn't have a life like that.

And Meredith—beautiful, intelligent, cool Meredith—still didn't know how much he was attracted to her. From the beginning, when she'd been so young and dating Tom. Even then—

"Stoney, *honey*," Karen said. "You don't *really* mean to stay in this hick town very long, do you? I miss you sooo much. And there's *nothing* here for you. It's so *boring*. And those boys you coach. I mean they're cute and all, but—"

"I like it here," Stoney said not quite truthfully. Colton had been a place to escape from when he was younger. He had few happy memories here. His return had been an impulsive act. Even now he hardly understood why he had come.

Karen leaned forward. She put her arm on the table. "Well, I mean it's small-town and all, and I *know* it's where you grew up, but you don't have to be here. You can still do commercials and things. And go to the parties and have fun...."

"That's not fun for me," Stoney said. "I don't want to do those things."

Karen's eyes narrowed. He watched dispassionately as the eye shadow she had so expertly applied folded in on itself. He knew his reaction to that crinkled color was unnecessarily harsh—Karen was, after all, a most spectacularly beautiful woman who knew how to make the most of herself. She'd drawn every male eye in the restaurant since they'd come in.

He was beginning to feel a little guilty for being so uninterested.

"It's that woman, isn't it?" Karen said flatly.

He looked away. "Maybe," he admitted slowly. He rested his hand on the table. "But not all."

There it was again—that flash of hurt in Karen's eyes, gone before he could really swear it was there. She reached over and put her hand atop his. Her fingers stroked his knuckles with slow, explicit suggestion. "Forget her," she said. "Take me home with you, Stoney. Let's go back to your place, and tomorrow morning you can drive me back to the city and see some of your old friends...." Her fingers continued their expert movement against his hand.

A long, slow shudder coursed through him as once again he felt his body begin to tense with need. He was beginning to feel disoriented and confused. Out of control. Maybe he should take Karen home. He knew all too well what it was like to lose himself in womanly softness, to lay his head against soft white breasts. A little forgetfulness for a moment.

Her hand still played against his. "Come on, Stoney," she said softly. "Let's go."

Then for a while maybe he wouldn't remember a clean-scrubbed face and hair the color of night silk. Maybe he wouldn't see dark eyes, telling him to keep away. Maybe he should take what Karen was offering and forget Meredith Blackmoore, at least until morning.

Right, a silent voice jeered. Fat chance. He hadn't forgotten her in six years, and there had been plenty of soft breasts. More than enough emptiness.

So that instead of agreeing, he heard himself saying with only a touch of betraying hoarseness in his voice, "Not tonight, Karen. Sorry."

Her hand stilled. She looked at him blankly.

"I didn't ask you to come here," he said, trying to soften the harshness of his words with a forced smile.

"You're turning me down?" Karen said.

Stoney shrugged, once again apologetic, uncomfortable. "I guess so, babe," he said. He looked out the window.

"I—I . . . Stoney—"

"I'll get you a room," he said. "In a motel or something."

"A motel room." Karen's voice had changed, grown flatter, thinner.

"I'm sorry," he said again, his discomfort growing by the second. He wished he were anywhere in the world but here. He wished he were still at the game this afternoon, seeing Meredith after all these years. He wished he'd talked with her longer.

And he was having another problem. For some reason he had the most unexpected compulsion to start grinning like some idiot schoolboy.

He was certainly one totally confused guy, he told himself. He needed to be alone. He needed to sort things out.

Wasn't that what he'd come to Colton to do? To sort out the life that hadn't made a hell of a lot of sense to him in a long time?

And to see Meredith, a little voice said. He'd come back to Colton to see Meredith Blackmoore.

"A motel room," Karen said again, her hand moving to touch the skin beneath her opened blouse. For a moment she looked as if she was going to cry.

He hoped like hell she wouldn't. He couldn't stand to be around crying women. Ever since he was a kid hearing his mother cry behind her closed bedroom door, a crying woman made him feel as if he should do something, fix something....

But thankfully Karen controlled herself. She took a deep, steadying breath and smiled at him bravely, which was almost worse, because for a minute he saw the little girl Karen had been, before the collagen and the designer clothes and the sweet perfumes and the fast life and the body that had been willing for more men than him.

"What are you doing anyway," he said to Karen, "coming out here in the middle of nowhere chasing a man like me? Don't you think you deserve better than this? Don't you want more than a one-night stand in a boring small town where there's no one around but strangers?"

"Sure," she snapped at him. "I looked for Prince Charming just yesterday, but—"

"And why do you talk like that? Like you don't believe in anything anymore? How old are you anyway? Twenty-one? Twenty-two? You've got a lifetime ahead of you. Why don't you go after something important? Why don't you find a man who'll treat you like something special? Who'll love only you?"

"I—" she began before her eyes teared in earnest. He looked away as she blinked furiously. She gave a little hiccuping laugh. "I guess," she said jerkily, "I thought maybe that man was you, Stoney." She made a little movement with her hand. "Silly of me, wasn't it?"

He was stunned. He rocked back in his chair. He moved a hand through his hair. "Me?" he said.

"My turn to apologize," she whispered.

He said the first words that came into his head, and he meant them, too. "You can do better than me."

She shook her head. Tears were flowing down her cheeks now, and she wiped them away with nervous, shaking fingers. "There's none better than you, Stoney Macreay. None. She's a lucky woman, this sister of one of your players."

"She doesn't think so," Stoney said. He stood abruptly. He didn't feel like grinning now. He felt worse than ever. "Let's go," he said. "Forget the motel room. I can fix you up at my place. On the sofa or something."

Karen shook her head, smiling gamely through her tears. "That's okay. I came from a small town, too—did you know that? I know how these people can be. Your...she'll know by noon that I spent the night at your place. Get me the room, Stoney. I'll survive."

Maybe that was all anyone could do, Stoney thought. He felt awkward, almost tender. He brushed his hand across Karen's cheek. "All right, babe," he said softly. "Come on."

He took her to the nicest motel in town and paid her bill in advance. "Can you get back tomorrow?" he asked.

"I'll manage," she told him. He bent down and kissed her one more time, and there was more honesty in that kiss than in all the ones that had gone before.

He left her then, and got in his fast little car and drove, through the night-dark streets of Colton, out into the country to the old run-down house—empty now—where he'd grown up. Then he drove back into town past the Blackmoore home where Meredith still lived with her daughter, then on past the old high school and the single movie theater. On his last loop through Colton, he passed Screens Alive!, the screen-printing business he knew

Meredith owned. Her car was still parked in front. There were lights on in the back of the shop.

His dashboard clock read well after midnight. And Meredith Blackmoore was still working.

For some reason that simple fact bothered him more than anything else that had happened today. What was she doing, he wondered, working so late? Surely her parents were helping her enough so that she didn't need to be working all hours just to survive. But then maybe, he thought darkly, she was one of those emancipated young women who would rather work than sleep. Or eat. Or be a mother to her lovely child.

No, he thought. That didn't fit with her protective behavior earlier today. And it really wasn't his business why she was working this time of night. She couldn't have made *that* more clear. If he was sensible, he'd just drive on by and not worry about Meredith Blackmoore.

He smiled grimly to himself. He'd just turned down the most lush, beautiful body that had come to Colton in a long time. Why start behaving sensibly now?

He pulled his car in next to Meredith's, got out and headed for the door.

The arrogant knock on the door shattered Meredith's concentration. She hadn't managed to get to work until about ten, and had been at it for over two hours now. She was bone weary.

The knock came again—three sharp *rat-a-tat*s sounding impatient and demanding in the silence of her shop.

Exhaustion caused her hands to shake slightly as she put down the spot cure, debating whether or not to answer the summons.

It was late, after all. And she was alone.

Once again the knock came, louder. "Meredith!" she heard. "It's me. Stoney."

Relief at the familiar voice washed through her. A quick spark of anger followed. And then there was something else that felt, strangely enough, like anticipation.

Stoney Macreay. Here. A glance at the clock reminded her of how late it was and how much she still had to do.

Why was he here?

She could think of a few reasons, all right. None of them comforting.

What had happened to his blonde?

She reminded herself that just this afternoon she had vowed to have nothing more to do with him. But that did seem a lifetime away as she stood here alone in her shop in the middle of the night.

He was rattling the doorknob now. She walked to the door and stared at it for a few seconds. She took two deep, calming breaths before turning the dead bolt and opening the door about three inches.

"What do you want?" she asked, pleased that she sounded so quiet and assured.

Her innocently worded question seemed to catch Stoney by surprise, and for a moment he just stared at her. The night shadows made his eyes seem dark, mysterious. His body was stretched and taut. Meredith felt her control begin to slip. Her cheeks grew hot.

Then he laughed, the sound low and huskily mocking. "I don't really think you want me to answer that. Maybe we should settle for the obvious instead. Can I come in?"

"Why?"

"I noticed the light. I thought maybe you'd like some help. Doing whatever you're doing."

"No, thanks." She shook her head and tried to close the door, but he blocked it with his foot. He put his hand up on the doorjamb.

"I don't want your help, Stoney," she repeated.

"Hey," he replied, too easily rejecting her rejection. "Truce, Meredith. What have I ever done to you?" When she didn't answer, he continued a little sternly, "Whatever it is, maybe I can make it better by helping you now."

He was right, of course. He had never actually done anything to her. She had treated him badly today because he was Tom's brother, and for no other reason. But when he'd wanted to talk with Tess, she'd been so suddenly afraid. She was conscious of something else—of the way she felt around him—had always felt. "Stoney, I—"

"How much longer are you going to be here?"

She answered him in spite of herself. "Another couple of hours, but you don't know anything about screen printing and—"

"Maybe not, but wouldn't another pair of hands make it all go faster? Whatever it is?"

His question cut through her confusion, and she actually thought about it. Help *would* be nice. She was so tired. By herself she had another three hours to go. The price, she knew, of spending the day with her daughter.

Stoney smiled his luxuriously seductive smile. "Come on, Meredith. Let me in."

How many times in the past months had she sworn to herself that she would have nothing to do with Stoney Macreay? How many times had she made that promise to herself just today?

Yet here she was, actually considering his suggestion.

Maybe it was sheer delight at the very thought of having someone here to help her. Maybe it was weariness clouding her thought processes. Maybe it was the strange anticipation she'd felt just moments before. Maybe it was the unexpectedness of it all—his arriving here, like this, at night, when she was alone.

Whatever it was, feeling disoriented and totally out of control, she opened the door and stepped aside. "All right. If you're fool enough to want to work instead of sleep at this time of night, who am I not to take advantage of such an opportunity?" Then she ruined the lightness of her words by blurting, "But don't think of trying anything, Stoney."

Where had those words come from? Surely she hadn't really spoken them aloud.

His face remained carefully blank as he took the door from her hands and shut it gently. "I'm not dangerous, Meredith." His smile was still in place as he said lightly, "I'm just attracted. To you." His tone was mild, as if he were merely talking about the weather or something. But she wasn't fooled. Her heart seemed to be performing some mad race of its own.

Again she remembered the blonde. "What happened to..." Her voice trailed off and she stood there, embarrassed at the words she was about to utter.

But Stoney knew who she meant. "Didn't stay." He shrugged.

"Must've broke your heart," she said.

He looked down and placed a hand over his chest. "Nope. It's still there. One piece." He glanced up and met her gaze directly. "Not a problem," he said.

The air thrummed around them. She felt dizzy. How had this happened? she wondered dazedly. In spite of everything—her resolves, her avoidance, her fear—she was standing in her shop listening to Stoney Macreay tell her he was attracted to her. That he was a free agent. Totally available.

So, God help her, was she.

And he knew it.

Abruptly she turned from him. "I'm working back here," she said, her tone only a little breathless.

Silently, with only the tiniest smile of victory curving his lips, Stoney followed her past the front desk where her secretary, Rose, usually sat, past Meredith's computer sitting atop a second desk, on past the big flat drawers of art files and the long table on which was laid out some art copy. She took him through the door which led to her actual "shop"—the room with the concrete floor and the three presses and two long ovens, and shelves with various materials hugging the walls.

It didn't take long for Meredith to show Stoney how to help her. He held the spot cure while she put shirt after shirt on the press, rotating it in order to apply the four colors the job demanded.

"When the pile stacks up at the end of the oven," she told Stoney, "take a break and fold the shirts into groups of twelve. Keep count on the paper there." She pointed to a sheet with scribblings already on it.

"Fun Run shirts," Stoney commented, looking at the pile of finished shirts already stacked on a table beside the longest oven.

"Uh-huh. Shelby Winters wants them by tomorrow so they can go on sale in the market."

"Don't you have people that usually do this for you?"

"Sure. Two of them. But lately this new salesman that I hired has been bringing in more work than we can handle. And one of my printers has been sick. In order to even make an attempt at keeping up, I come in sometimes at night."

"Owner's privilege," Stoney said wryly.

"Right."

"Since when?"

"What?"

"How long have you owned this place?"

She shrugged. "My dad helped me get it when I was eighteen. After I graduated from high school."

She was in motion now, working steadily. Out of the corner of her eye, she saw Stoney silently mouth the word *eighteen*. His eyes were dark and serious.

Meredith tried to concentrate on her work. It was tedious stuff, placing the shirts on the platen, squeegeeing each color through its individual screen, spot-curing with a hand-held electric heater after each application so the colors wouldn't run. And now, even though with Stoney's help it was going faster, she was more than ever aware of the time.

But he also made her aware of more than the time. Standing next to her, dressed in the same casual jeans and too big cream-colored Shaker-knit sweater he'd been wearing at the game, he looked impossibly beautiful to her—somehow larger than life, a golden prince, a mystical hero. He'd changed the atmosphere in her shop just by being here. Even the dim corners seemed to vibrate with some knowing electrical charge.

She put another shirt on the platen and attempted, not very successfully, to just ignore him.

"Are you ever sorry you didn't go to medical school like you wanted?" Stoney asked.

His words pierced her. That he should remember their long-ago conversation staggered her. Memories of that night, and all that went with it, washed through her. She shoved the memories away.

Turning from him, she shrugged. "Sure," she said. "Sometimes I'm sorry. But I've been thinking of still doing it."

"Good," he said approvingly, and she felt suddenly better.

"Tess is a beautiful child," he said, changing the subject.

More of her tension melted away. "Yes."

"You've been a good mother to her."

"Thanks. Though I couldn't have done it without Mom and Dad."

He nodded in silent acceptance of her statement. For a while after that they didn't say much, just worked steadily together. After a bit Meredith felt a strangeness settle over her, and she grew all quiet inside. Yet the silence wasn't exactly peaceful—it was more of a *knowing*. Like the kind of knowing you had that a storm was coming in the hush preceding it.

She inhaled the faint residual odor of some manly cologne Stoney had used earlier in the day. When she turned to him for help from the spot cure, she couldn't meet his eyes, lest she give away the incredibly alive awareness she felt. She looked at his hands instead. His nails were neatly kept, his knuckles lean and loose jointed.

"Roger told me you're still living at home," he said conversationally.

"That's right."

"What grade is Tess in?"

"First." A testiness had crept into her tone.

"How does she like school?"

"She likes it fine."

A flash of irritation sparked in his eyes. "Look," he said, "aren't there any faster ways of doing this?"

"Faster and more expensive. We do all right with this equipment." She added with exaggerated sweetness, "Bored already?"

"Actually I was just wondering how many times you've done this in the last four years."

"Thousands. Millions." She kept her head high. She was proud of what she'd accomplished.

He put a hand on her shoulder, and a little whoosh of air escaped her lips. "It's just that I'm totally impressed, Meredith," he said gently. "You really are—" he paused, as if searching for the right word "—magnificent."

She felt a warm blush begin to spread upward across her cheeks and blinked furiously. She couldn't think of anything to say. They continued working until at last the time came when she reached for the next shirt, only to find there wasn't one.

"Finished," she said. She felt incredibly breathless and shy. She forced herself to turn to him and gave him what she hoped was a cool look of self-possession. "Thanks for the help."

"You're welcome." His smile was crooked and self-deprecating. He was such a mass of contradictions—the big hero with the lost-little-boy smile.

Very tentatively she smiled back.

"Want to stop for coffee somewhere?" he suggested.

Her eyes flew to his. His expression had changed somehow. He'd been so laid-back, so nonthreatening. Now there was a disconcerting openness in the way his eyes searched her features, an open hunger in the blaze that grew in the back of his eyes.

She looked at the clock. It was ten minutes after two. Two hours ago she had been almost dropping from exhaustion. But she wasn't tired now. Just the opposite— she felt filled with energy. She felt invincible with it. Adrenaline raced through her.

So that she almost said yes.

Stoney must have read that answer in her eyes, because his beautiful mouth curved upward in his long, slow smile. "Hurry up," he said.

She jerked her gaze from his, more shaken than she wanted to admit. Stoney Macreay looked at all his women just like that, she was sure. His eyes grew opaque, bedroom cloudy. She'd be a fool to fall for a look like that. She ignored the weakness in her lower body and splayed her hands against the now barren platen. "I...can't," she managed to say, shaking her head. "It's too late."

"Meredith—"

"No," she said again, more firmly.

He was standing in front of her, so she couldn't very easily get past him to the door. He stared at her, his look challenging now, almost angry. He was no longer smiling. "Why not?"

How could she explain? She was sure Stoney Macreay had women going with him all times of the day and night. But she would never be one of them, no matter how alive he made her feel. She had Tess to think about, and her own future.

He reached out and touched her face, the gentleness of his movement catching her unaware. She stared at him silently.

"I've thought about you," he said.

"How many times, Stoney?" she asked him starkly. "Twice? Three times? In between how many other women?"

He gave his wry, twisted smile, which didn't quite reach his eyes. "Ouch," he said. Then he added, dropping his smile, "Not like that at all, Meredith. Many times. Too many. I'd catch myself thinking of the shy, beautiful girl my brother had—"

"Stop!"

He seemed a loss for words. Finally he said, his voice low and deep, "Try an experiment, Meredith?"

"What kind of experiment?" she asked distrustfully.

"This," he said. Then he slid his hand down her arm and pulled her to him, buried his other hand in her hair, lowered his head and kissed her.

Shock spread like wildfire through her veins, holding her momentarily still. His lips stayed on hers—light, questioning little nibbles—not going any farther, giving her time to respond to him, to tell him what to do next.

Dear Lord, she thought in that part of her brain that was still functioning, but he's good at this.

She should jerk away, she told herself. She should freeze up like ice, as she'd done during the kisses of other men she had known. She should still the sudden pounding of her heart, she should—

She gave a great shudder, leaned her idiot heart into him and silently asked for more.

He gave.

It wasn't like any kisses she'd ever known. Certainly not like Tom's had been.

His lips were warm and dry and terribly alive. They sucked and pulled, then grew hard and demanding. One of his hands buried itself in her hair—the other pulled her close against his body. And if she lived to be a hundred, she was absolutely positive nothing could ever compare to what she was feeling at this moment. Comprehension was exploding within her; this was what poets sang about, what writers tried to explain. This was what caused people to lose their senses, their inhibitions. And with good reason. She understood everything now. Because this feel of his lips against hers, this opening of mouths and touching of hands, this—this *intimacy* of feeling and need was surely hunger and feast, longing and fulfillment, question and answer all rolled into one. And such heat, such exquisite, glowing, melting, beckoning heat—

He lifted his head. "Nice," he said, his voice husky and male and supremely triumphant. "Very."

Nice, she thought numbly. Nice, she repeated in her head. Stoney Macreay thought kissing her was *nice.*

She pulled herself together. Which was a much harder feat than it should have been.

She realized too late that she was trembling from head to foot. Somehow her hands had crept up around Stoney's neck. For this nice kiss.

What a ninny she was, to be in a swoon over a kiss from Stoney Macreay. Especially a *nice* one. She reminded herself of the innumerable women Stoney had kissed, more than kissed. She told herself what she should feel: angry, used, indignant. She should probably slap him or something.

But instead, all she really felt was confused. And strangely fluid. And unfinished.

And underneath all of it, hurt.

"Stoney," she said. "Don't play with me."

His eyes darkened. "Is that what you think I'm doing?"

"Yes," she said proudly. "But I'm not a game. And neither is Tess."

"I never thought you were."

She hadn't meant to make him mad. But she could see she had in the way he tensed. In the way his hand rough-combed his hair in a gesture she was beginning to recognize. His golden lion's eyes were as dark as she'd ever seen them. The color of a storm, she reminded herself. Time to take shelter.

"Finish up what you have to do," he said, his tone curt, leashed in. Then he began, "Meredith..." She thought he would say more, but he merely shook his head, as if shaking off some confusion, and added, "I'll follow you home."

"I've done this a hundred times, Stoney. There's no need for you to play the chaperone." Oh, she was cool now. Cool as ice.

"There's every need. I want to make sure you're safe."

"No," she said. Beneath the coolness, she felt hot tears pushing to get out. "Please go."

And she thought he did. He went out the door, and she shut off the equipment and the lights, checked the locks and started to take boxes of printed shirts out to her car. That was when she knew Stoney hadn't left—he was sitting in his sports car parked next to hers, watching her. When she came out the door with her second box, Stoney was at her side in a flash, swearing under his breath, taking the shirts from her. She didn't try to fight him. She just silently handed him the box and went back for a third. Then, after they had her car loaded up, he followed her to Shelby Winters's house, where he helped her unload the shirts in Shelby's unlocked garage. When she moved to get into her now empty car, he stopped her. "This isn't a game," he said. "I wasn't playing."

She had no reply. By this time, a part of her didn't care whether he was playing or not. Now that she'd got used to the idea that he thought the kiss merely nice, a part of her actually wanted him to kiss her again, to reassure her that she could really *feel* like that, really *want* like that.

But she didn't tell Stoney that. He was a game player, after all, no matter what he said. And he played to win. He'd recognize a weakness when he saw one. "Good night," she whispered instead.

She thought he would touch her again, there in Shelby Winters's garage, so she turned from him quickly.

"Good night, sweet Merry," she heard him say.

Then she got in her car, and he got in his. And true to his word, he did follow her, all the way home.

She pulled into her parents' driveway, turned off her engine and pushed the button that darkened her headlights. Stoney's car was waiting on the street, its engine still running. Without looking his way, she got out of her car and let herself in the side door of the house.

But it wasn't until she entered her own room and flicked the light switch that she heard Stoney rev his engine and drive away.

Chapter Five

The next morning Meredith woke late and unrested.

Sunday, was her first thought. No work today.

Then her second thought came: *Stoney Macreay kissed me last night.*

She moaned.

And then she allowed it to come: pleasure. Deep, sensual, heretofore unknown pleasure.

She threw her arm over her head and lay still, thinking about it, experiencing it. Last night, long after his car had pulled away, she'd felt it—the tingling, the trembling, the wonder. For the first time since she could remember, undressing for bed had been more than a simple, mindless act. She had accomplished it slowly, stripping off first one piece of clothing, then another, imagining with exquisite longing what it would be like to undress for a man like Stoney Macreay.

When she'd finally slept, she'd dreamed of him.

Then the warm morning sunshine streaming in through her bedroom window brought with it a firmer reality. She tried to examine things objectively. Their kiss had obviously meant a lot more to her than to Stoney. This shouldn't bother her, she told herself staunchly. Stoney was, after all, the kind of man who took physical desire and physical satisfaction for granted. She'd known that years ago, and she knew it now.

She wasn't like him—that was all. So it was only natural that the kiss should mean so much more to her. Since the night so many years ago that had produced Tess, she had been sure that certain female feelings were never going to happen to her. Ever. Stoney's kiss had blown that theory to kingdom come. His kiss had been a startling revelation, an incredible awakening.

She wasn't different, as she had feared for so long. She, too, could experience the feelings of being a woman. An elated grin crept across her face. She felt giddy with relief. She wasn't incapable of finding pleasure in closeness, in a kiss. Even now she felt like swooning. She wanted to stay by herself for hours, to savor at length the sensations Stoney had aroused.

How do people go on living, knowing that they can feel such things? she wondered. How does anyone ever get anything done? How do people stay focused? How do they achieve things?

She thought of her mother. Always so serene, so peaceful. So content. Did she feel like this sometimes? Did she crave her husband's touch? Her husband's kisses?

Is that what made her mother so content with her life? An unending supply of kisses and more?

Meredith thought of the secret private looks her mother sometimes gave to her father, letting all who saw know that for Kathleen, happiness was being married to Hudson Blackmoore.

So what's wrong with me? Meredith wondered restlessly. Because even after last night, even with the resulting hunger still throbbing in her veins—or maybe because of it—she couldn't forget what she'd been thinking before Stoney showed up. About dreams and hopes and real aspirations. Maybe she wasn't like her mother. Maybe marriage would never be the pot of gold at the end of her rainbow. She was just beginning to come alive. There were things she wanted to do. Places she wanted to go. She thought of her daughter—she loved Tess with all her heart, yet even that wasn't enough to fill all the longing spaces inside her.

Stoney Macreay would understand what she meant. She was sure of it. He probably didn't want to be married, either. She thought he'd played around far too much to be satisfied with just one woman, ever.

Which wasn't exactly the most reassuring thought she'd ever had.

Maybe if she'd had more experience, she'd understand things better. That one time in Tom's car had been it for her. She'd never really wanted sex again, never come near allowing any man that intimacy again. Even though she'd told herself repeatedly that what he'd done to her wasn't really important. That she'd got over it fully. But she'd never told anyone the truth about that night. She'd never shared with anyone exactly how Tess was conceived.

How could she, when she could barely think of it herself?

She wasn't really over anything, she admitted now. Not Tom's violence, not being sixteen and pregnant, not raising a child without an acknowledged father.

Ever since the night Tess was conceived, Meredith could barely think about kissing a man or touching him....

Until last night.

Now she could think about it, all right. And think and think and think about it. It was only the irony of the ages that the man who had somehow got her past that hurdle and given her those responses would be someone so totally inappropriate as Stoney Macreay.

It wasn't an easy thought, in the midst of all that unexpected pleasure. If she wasn't careful, she'd mess up her life again, just as she'd done six years before. Only worse this time, because she was older and wiser and her heart would be involved.

Another jock hero, she mocked herself. Tom's big brother, for heaven's sake. Another all-American guy. You would think she'd learned enough not to be caught in that trap twice.

She stood up and started to get dressed with jerky, hurried movements. Everything was a jumble—she hardly knew what to think.

Last night.

Bemusedly she put her hands on her heart and did a dreamy twirl around her room. She'd felt so suddenly alive. So *womanly*. She really didn't care that Stoney wasn't the man for her, or that her rational mind told her Stoney lived a life in total disharmony with her own.

She didn't want to be rational, so she wasn't.

She just wanted him to kiss her again.

So what if his whole life had been concentrated on being the jock hero, on winning things—games, popularity, women. Even now, as a coach, winning was the thing. She'd seen him after a game. She knew what he was like.

But she didn't have to like what he liked in order for him to teach her things—things she was dying to know.

She wanted to be kissed like that again. She wanted the reassurance that she could enjoy it again, like that. She wanted to know that she hadn't made it up, hadn't remembered it wrong.

It was all so new. So intoxicating, so unbearably desirable.

Oh! Oh! Oh! she thought, putting her hands to her cheeks. What was happening to her? Suddenly it wasn't all pleasant, this new discovery. It was scary. Terrifying. What if this new twist threw things out of whack? Caused her balancing act to fall apart, so that she lost control?

Worse—what if she was never kissed like that ever again?

She couldn't stay up here mooning about it, she decided. She needed to be around people, to experience the familiar. She would think about all this later. She needed to think about other things now. Other people.

She wanted to see Tess.

She was opening Tess's bedroom door before she remembered that her mother had taken Tess to church today. Which thought brought her mood spiraling down as she accepted her usual burden of guilt. She should be the one taking her daughter to church. She should have more time for Tess, be teaching Tess what was important and what wasn't.

Meredith's parents had always been there for her; she should be there for Tess. That was the way life worked, wasn't it?

Suddenly she was profoundly confused. How she was living, what she was accomplishing, seemed forever in conflict with how she wanted to live, what she wanted to accomplish. Only her determination kept her in control.

She definitely wasn't in control today. Stoney Macreay had seen to that.

She had to get out of her room. Away from her silent single bed. Away from her thoughts.

She went downstairs to find her father and found him sitting at the kitchen table, drinking a cup of coffee and reading the Sunday newspaper. She poured herself a cup and sat opposite him.

He looked at her over his paper. "Good morning, Sunshine," he said.

He'd always called her "Sunshine" since she was a small child. She smiled at him, feeling somehow relieved. "Hi, Dad." See, she told herself, nothing's changed. All those thoughts I was having upstairs—they mean nothing. Everything's all right now.

"Work late last night?" her father asked.

"Yeah. Had to get the Fun Run shirts done."

He went back to his paper. She stared at the dark liquid in her cup. She felt her momentary peace leave her.

"Dad," she said impulsively.

"Hmm?"

"I've been thinking. About my future."

He looked at her, an eyebrow raised questioningly.

"You know what a time I'm having at the shop. I need to expand. Only...every time I think about it I get so darned depressed."

"Depressed?" Her father sounded surprised. "I'd think you'd be proud, Meredith."

"I am, Dad. Only...sometimes I wonder if I'm doing what I'm supposed to be doing, you know? Sometimes I think about going back to school."

"School? You mean college?"

She nodded. "Remember when I wanted to be a doctor, just like you? It was all I could think about, until..." her voice faded away.

"Until you had Tess."

Again she nodded. "I guess I thought that I had to rearrange everything to make sure Tess was happy. And you and Mom were so helpful, and made everything so easy—"

"It wasn't easy for you," her father interrupted. "If you don't remember that, I do." He paused. "It still isn't easy, is it, Meredith?"

Her eyes suddenly filled with tears. She thought of always having to explain about Tess's nonfather. She thought of the long hours at work. "No," she said, fighting the stupid self-pity. "I guess not. But Tess is worth it, Dad."

"Of course she is, Sunshine."

"She really is happy."

"Yes."

"I suppose it's been difficult for you and Mom, though. I don't want you to think I'm not grateful." She was speaking jerkily now. "But I think it's time for me to move on, that's all. Take charge of my own life."

Unexpectedly her father smiled. "Sunshine," he said. "It's all right. We knew this day would come. Though it'll be hard on your mother, it's not unexpected. She saw the writing on the wall long ago."

"What do you mean?"

"I mean she's already prepared herself for your leaving."

"She has?"

"She loves you, Meredith. She wants you to be happy. You haven't been happy here. We've both known that. You've been... enduring. Not that you haven't done well. You have—and both your mother and I are filled with pride for you. But it's time for you and Tess to go. And time for us to let you go."

"Oh, Dad," Meredith said.

"We'll help you with tuition. I always planned to, before."

"You helped me with Screens Alive. That was enough, Dad."

He touched her cheek lightly. "Now, no more of that. You paid me back, every penny. We can help you with your college education."

Meredith shook her head. She leaned forward in her chair. "I want to do it myself, Dad. If I can. I think I can sell the business for enough to support Tess and me for the next four years, if I work in the summers. And after that, when I need to go on to medical school, we'll see. I think being an older student and a mother will open some financial doors for me.''

Sometime during this speech, Meredith's heart began to pound. She had placed both hands on the table; she discovered she was wringing them together. And yet, in spite of her obvious tension, she was feeling something else, something so brave and wonderful and expansive that she could have cried out with the joy of it. I can do it, she thought wonderingly. I really can do what I said.

Time to move on. To grow.

''All right,'' her father said. She'd never seen his eyes more tender, his smile more proud. ''Go for it, Meredith.''

There was a knock on the kitchen door. ''Anybody home?'' It was Roger's girlfriend, Beth. Seeing Meredith and her father, Beth sauntered in.

It was an indication of Beth's commitment to Roger that she felt so at home with his family. She often came around, whether Roger was there or not. Although today Roger was home, as far as Meredith knew. Most likely still in bed. Roger was a notoriously late sleeper on Sunday mornings.

''Hi,'' Beth said. She sat down at the table and started to read the funnies.

Meredith's father gave Meredith an amused look. Meredith shrugged, fighting back a tremulous smile. ''I think I'll go for a walk,'' she said, finding it impossible to sit still, to stay inside. A whole wide world waited for her out the door. ''I have some things to think about.''

''You do that,'' her father said. ''It's time for me to start making dinner, anyway.'' It was a long-standing Sunday tradition that her father made the Blackmoore Sunday dinner.

''I'll go with you,'' Beth said.

Meredith felt a pang of annoyance. Hadn't she just said she wanted to think? Beth was not usually so obtuse. But Meredith gave her brother's girlfriend a smile just the same. "All right," she said.

At first they walked in silence, Meredith lost in her thoughts, Beth seemingly content to match Meredith's strides. From time to time Meredith glanced at Beth. Not for the first time, she recognized what a pretty girl Beth was. Long blond hair. Tall. Straight, even features. And truly beautiful eyes. Roger definitely had good taste.

She swallowed the green monster, envy. Beth had her whole life ahead of her. She hadn't made Meredith's stupid mistakes.

The area around the Blackmoore home included some of the nicest houses in town. The homes all had large, spacious, well-tended yards. A wide sidewalk connected the curling, darkly paved driveways. The air itself was autumn clean and crisp—beckoning, challenging. Meredith found it all almost unbearably nostalgic. I'm going to do it, she thought. I'm going to do what I always wanted to do. I'm going to be what I always wanted to be.

She wanted to talk with Stoney. She wanted to tell him what she'd been thinking.

"Meredith," Beth said.

"Hmm?"

"When you were my age, did you, uh—"

Meredith looked at Beth. The girl's face was blushing rosily, and her eyes were downcast.

"What, Beth?"

"Oh, never mind." Beth kicked a stone on the sidewalk.

But Meredith's curiosity was aroused. "Something on your mind?" she said.

"Not really," Beth said.

"Everything okay between you and Roger?"

"Sure." They walked on. Meredith took deep, cleansing breaths while her mind wandered from thought to thought. She wasn't thinking about her future now; she was again reliving Stoney's kiss.

"Well..." Beth spoke again. "We're having a few problems. Nothing major, though. Just little things."

"How little?"

"Nothing much."

"Hmm," Meredith said vaguely.

"But I did want to know something," Beth said.

"What?"

"Well...When was the first time you...I mean, when did you decide to...you know...make love with a man?" The last words came out in a rush, and Beth's face was really flaming now.

Meredith stopped, stunned. She stared at Beth. "Are you and Roger—"

Beth shook her head vigorously. "No. At least, not yet."

"Not yet," Meredith repeated flatly.

"But he wants to, you know. He's been asking. He wants more than...just kisses. And I thought I needed to talk with someone. Before we did anything."

Dear God, Meredith thought, appalled at this turn in the conversation. Who does she think I am, some counselor at the birth-control clinic? She should be talking to her mother, not me.

As if reading her thoughts, Beth burst out in near panic, "Oh please, please, *please* don't tell my parents. Or yours, either. Say you won't. Everybody's doing it, you know. It's just that I'm not sure—"

"Not sure of what?"

"If I'm ready."

"Or if you want it at all?" Meredith suggested dryly.

Beth nodded, a little forlornly. "I mean, I *love* Roger, but..."

How curious, that sixteen-year-old Beth should be so sure of something like that. "What does that mean, to love him?" Meredith asked.

"Well, I mean he's been my steady for over a year now, and I spend all my free time with him. And we're already talking about getting married."

Married, Meredith thought helplessly, remembering her own thoughts on the subject just a short while ago. What should she say now? For the life of her, she couldn't think of anything, but she was determined to try.

"Beth," she said, floundering. "What do you want to do with your life?"

"What do you mean?" Beth said.

"What do you want out of life? What do you want to do? Accomplish?"

"I want what most girls want, I suppose," Beth said slowly. "To have a home of my own. A husband. Children."

"Is that all?" Meredith asked. "What about besides all that?"

"Besides?"

"Yeah. Do you want to be anything? Are you interested in anything?"

"I'm interested in lots of things." This obviously wasn't the direction Beth had expected this conversation to take. She shook her head in almost tentative defiance. "Right now I'm interested in Roger."

"I see. And what about life after Roger?" Meredith said gently. She was beginning to feel incredibly old. "What if the two of you don't get married? On the other hand, what if you do? Beth, do you know how many marriages actually make it? Do you understand how many women—and men—get married to the wrong person? You're not even out of high school yet. Isn't it a bit early to be making decisions like this?"

Beth didn't reply. They'd come quite a distance, all downhill. The hardest part was yet to come. "Let's turn around," Meredith suggested. Silently Beth obeyed.

Meredith felt herself sighing. She supposed she had to say something. Give some kind of guidance. "Beth," she tried. "You know Tess is five years old, don't you?"

"Yeah," Beth said.

"And I'm twenty-two. I guess you can figure out the arithmetic."

"Uh-huh."

"And you know who Tess's father was?"

"Roger told me."

"I was sixteen, Beth. I had plans. Dreams, really. But I let Tom do something with me that I wasn't ready for. I've thought about it a lot since." Meredith paused, trying to think of ways to put what had happened to her in words Beth would understand. "He was wrong, you know. What he did was wrong. He believed he was old enough. Mature enough. He was all raging hormones, and he mistook that for divine right or something. But it was a lie—all of us bought into a big lie that you can..."

"Not everybody gets pregnant," Beth said, angry defensiveness making her voice almost snide. "And not everybody's boyfriend would deny his own child." Beth made Tom's betrayal sound like Meredith's fault.

Meredith felt anger riot through her, but she clamped it down tight. Beth was only a child. "No," she agreed, "not everybody's boyfriend would deny his own child. But as a general rule, adolescent boys aren't great father material. And even if you don't get pregnant, you're still fooling around with stuff you shouldn't. I know how it is—the parties, the booze, the drugs. Are you and Roger into all that, Beth?"

Beth wouldn't look at Meredith. "Not exactly," she said, but her voice was small. Meredith's heart sank.

"Is Roger drinking?"

Beth took so long to say anything Meredith already had her answer. "Not very much," she said at last, in a whisper.

"Are you?" Meredith said.

"No! At least, only once or twice."

Right, Meredith thought cynically. "How about drugs?" she asked.

Beth's eyes got red, and she looked away.

"What's Roger doing?" This time Meredith didn't try to hide her anger. "Breaking all the rules like every dumb jock in this town has done for years? Who does he think he is, someone immortal? That none of this can touch him? And when he asks you for sex, is he thinking of you? Or only of that something in him that demands release? Is he in control at all? Is he caring about you? About your future?"

"I don't know," Beth practically wailed. "Sometimes I think he is. But other times . . ."

"You don't have to do it!" Meredith said. "You don't have to give in! You can choose the time and place of your own initiation. Which I hope is a long time from now, Beth. You can even wait until you're married, if you want to. People used to do that all the time."

"But they weren't always happy—" Beth began.

"The kids I remember having back-room sex six years ago weren't happy, either. They were more like *frantic*. If Roger *loves* you, he won't push you on this."

"But what if he finds someone else? What if he doesn't want me anymore?"

"Listen to what you're saying! As if your happiness is all tied up in what Roger thinks of you. It's more important what you think of yourself. Do what's best for you, and let the chips fall where they may. If you lose Roger over this, then something is desperately wrong. Besides," Meredith said, deliberately lightening her tone, "if he treats you badly, I'll personally mash that boy's face in. I'll cut off his ears and break his nose."

Beth cracked a very small smile. The walk uphill was more strenuous, and they were both panting slightly. Meredith stopped under a huge old oak tree and took Beth's hand. "Beth, maybe you came to the wrong person," she said. "Maybe I don't know how to help you at all. But I remember my mother talking about how happy she was in high school—those were some of the best years of her life. And I remember thinking later that she must have lived in a different time, on a different planet. Because high school wasn't happy for me, especially after I began to realize what was really going on. It was scary. I was always confused. Things were going on all around me that I didn't understand, and nobody seemed to have any answers. I wasn't so good, you know. I have Tess, don't I? But if I had it to do over again, I would go to class and study and keep my grades high, and not date at all. I wouldn't get involved in any of that stuff. Even if it meant I was lonely. Even if I didn't have any friends. Because you know what?"

"What?" Beth said.

"When it was all said and done, none of my friends could help me raise Tess. Or finish high school. Or make a life for myself. One or two stood by me, but what kind of wisdom can a sixteen-year-old kid have? In the end it was my mom and dad that helped. And I remember that time as all craziness. All stupidity. All nothing." Meredith's voice was bitter.

"Roger and me, we're not like that—"

"No?" Meredith was skeptical.

"No," Beth said, challenging now.

"You're sure?"

"Yes."

It's hopeless, Meredith thought. There's no way I can make her understand. "Well, just remember this," she said. "You don't have to barter yourself for anybody's love. Not even my hotshot brother's. If he even knows how to love yet, which I doubt. You don't have to offer yourself."

Suddenly Beth was blinking away tears. In an instant Meredith melted and put her arm around Beth's shoulders. "Look inside yourself for your answers," she said. "You won't find them anyplace else. Certainly not in the lives of your friends."

"I don't know," Beth said uncertainly.

They walked back to the house. Meredith's mom was just driving in with Tess. "You going to come in?" Meredith asked.

Beth shook her head. "Look, you won't tell Roger I talked to you, will you?"

"No," Meredith said.

"Or my parents? Or yours?"

"Hey. Don't make me a part of all this. I won't be part of the sickness. Not anymore. The only promise I'll make is that if I do talk to someone, I'll let you know."

Beth was not reassured. "I thought you were my friend!" she cried.

"Trust me," Meredith said.

But with a choked sound, Beth turned and ran down the street. Deeply troubled, Meredith went to join her mother and Tess, who had come home from a quiet morning in church.

Later that day Meredith took Tess down to the park for a picnic. She'd packed a light lunch of sandwiches, chips and juice. The day had remained consistently beautiful. The sun was bright and hot upon their cheeks.

After they had eaten, Meredith joined Tess on the tall swings. For some time they enjoyed the rhythmical up-and-down motion of the swings, pumping their legs in unison, giggling like sisters when they were able to match each other's movements.

Finally, breathless, they leaped from the still-moving swings onto the sand below.

"Mom?"

"What, darling child?"

"You're the best mom in the whole world."

Meredith grinned hugely. "And you're the best daughter."

Tess's gaze shifted, and her eyes widened. "Hi, Coach," she said.

Meredith froze there in the sand beneath the now gently moving swing. Slowly she turned her head. Stoney was standing there, dressed in black running shorts and a white T-shirt, panting slightly. Sweat glistened on his legs and arms.

"Hi, Tess," he said, but his eyes were on Meredith.

Meredith sat up, keeping a wary eye on the swing. Stoney caught it and held it still, before holding out a hand to help her up.

His hand was warm and damp. As she rose to her feet, her eyes fell to Stoney's right leg.

A scar angled down his leg and across his knee. It glowed obscenely pink against his tanned, muscled upper leg.

"My battle scar," Stoney said. "The wars of my life."

"Oh," Meredith said.

"Did it hurt?" Tess asked. "When it happened?"

"Yes."

"Does it hurt now?"

"Yes."

"Why do you run, then?" Meredith asked sharply. "Why give yourself pain?"

Stoney smiled his crooked smile. "Why get up in the morning? Why not just give in and lay there, until one day passes into another and you've..."

Unconsciously Meredith reached out and touched the pulsing pink flesh. Stoney closed his eyes briefly. When he opened them, their gaze locked. "I don't let anyone touch me there," he said.

She jerked her hand away.

"But you can touch me anywhere you want, Meredith."

And she felt it again. Rushing, expanding, warm liquid fire through her bones and blood and heart. She opened her mouth slightly.

He made a sound in his throat.

"Coach," Tess said. "Will you teach me to play soccer?"

For a moment Stoney said nothing. Then, as if with great difficulty, he turned his head and smiled at Tess. "Sure," he said. His voice sounded hoarse, raspy.

"Right now? I've brought a ball."

Some of the tautness left his body. "Sure," he said again. "Tell me what you know already."

And they were off, Stoney and her daughter, laughing and dribbling and passing to each other. Meredith watched as Stoney showed her daughter how to better control the ball with her foot. How to bounce the ball on her knee. How to pass with greater strength.

"Mom!" Tess called again and again. "Watch me! Watch me!"

But more often it was Stoney that she watched. His body was lean and supple. His arms long and strong. And always his scar, pink and swollen, looking violently out of place on his leg.

She watched until she could no longer bear the golden beauty of him, the lean grace of him, the effortless way he charmed her daughter with his bantering smile and easy words. She closed her eyes and leaned her head back against the park bench she had sunk into. But still she heard Tess's laughter and Stoney's deep masculine chuckles.

She heard other sounds, too. The bees in the field next to them. The birds singing in the trees. The wind in the brightly colored autumn leaves.

Then they were there—Tess on one side of her, Stoney easing himself down on the other, his arm stretched out loosely behind her, his fingers feathering her neck. She smelled him now, the deep, manly scent of his body, combined with the aroma of his shaving cream.

"Did you see me, Mom? Did you?"

"Yes." Still she kept her eyes closed, feeling Stoney's closeness like a cocooning warmth from home.

"She's good," Stoney said.

Another time Meredith would ask him if he were just being kind. Now she wanted to drink him in. She remembered again how she felt when he kissed her, and she wanted to feel like that again.

"Are you going to come and see us play tomorrow?" he asked her. His knuckles were rubbing against her cheek, up and down, lightly. And the touch was enough to send her trembling.

"Meredith?"

Then she remembered Tom, years ago, calling her up. "Come see me play, Merry," he'd say. She'd gone then, and look where it got her.

She should tell Stoney no. She knew it as well as she knew the sun rose in the east each morning. She shouldn't let this continue. She shouldn't even see Stoney Macreay again—

"I'll be there," she said.

"Good," he replied, letting out a breath. "I'm glad, Meredith."

Then he rose from the bench, and she opened her eyes and stared at him. His eyes were on fire. He spread out his arms and bent down, placing one hand on either side of Tess and herself, encircling them. She thought he might kiss her, but he didn't, only gave them both one possessively all-embracing look before he straightened and, with a casual wave of his hand, jogged away from them, down the path. She was left with the smell of him in her nostrils, the feel of him on her skin and the sight of him burned into her memory.

"I like Coach," Tess said enthusiastically. "He's great."

Which saved Meredith from having to make any comment at all.

Colton's weekday soccer games were played early, because the soccer field wasn't lit. That meant a lot of parents couldn't make it until the game was half-over, Meredith's father included. But her mother was there. And they'd brought Tess, of course. Beth was there, too, but this time she sat well away from the family. With her friends.

Colton won. Another shutout, five to nothing. Meredith heard several parents making plans for the state championship. "We can do it this year," she heard one father say. "What with Stoney coaching and the kids we've got on board, no one will be able to stop us!"

Us, she thought. As if we're all down there playing on the field. As if all of our identities are caught up in the score of a game.

Stoney disengaged himself from his victorious team and congratulatory parents almost immediately, and came to her. He was dressed all in black today, which only set off his male blond beauty more. He was obviously pleased with the game; she could see it in his eyes, in his smile, in the way his body moved. All stretched out and taut. There was something about a man like Stoney, after a win. He became, somehow, more *male*. The civilized edges were peeled away, so that he revealed a different nature, more predatory, raw, basic. More sexual.

And she, fool that she was, was caught up in that male excitement. It was all she could do to sit there calmly, not letting him know that her blood was racing wildly, that once again she was feeling that rush of mad expectancy that had her world turned upside down, only this time it was stronger than before, more inviting, more terrifying. She felt the pull of him as an irresistible force. Decide for me, she thought almost wildly. Don't ask. Tell me what to do next. She sat, still and waiting, watching him from her spot on the bottom bleacher.

"Hello," he said, smiling down at her.

"Hello, Stoney," she said gravely back.

"You came," he said. His eyes were like the sun, burning her.

"I told you I would."

Roger came over. "Can I get a ride home with you?" he said obliviously to Meredith. He looked so friendly and open that the boy she had been discussing with Beth on Sunday could have been another person.

"Sure," she agreed, her eyes touching Roger only briefly before returning of their own accord to Stoney. He was watching her with steady intensity. Then, with a slight shudder she broke the spell and stood, looking around for Tess, who had, as usual, disappeared.

The crowd was leaving. All around her she could sense the excitement of the win, the jubilation of victory. She spotted Tess, chattering a million miles a minute with another young friend.

"Roger, go get your niece," Stoney ordered.

Roger looked surprised. "How come?"

"Just go," Stoney said. And Roger, looking at Stoney and Meredith with sudden understanding in his youthfully narrowed eyes, went.

"That wasn't necessary," Meredith said stiffly.

"I just wanted a few minutes with you, without your little brother breathing down our necks." Stoney was unrepentant.

She was going to speak, say something casual, but when Stoney put his hand on her arm, all the words stopped in her throat. Everything froze for her then, except the heat she felt from his touch.

Stoney smiled his crooked smile in acknowledgment. He seemed to be vibrating now, and she with him. "Meredith."

"What?" Her voice sounded strange, hoarse.

"I'm glad you came today," he said. Then he bent his head and brushed his lips lightly against her own.

It wasn't much, that kiss. Certainly nothing like what they'd done the other night. But her heart stopped, just the same.

And then, his eyes lidded and his face suddenly slack, he did it again.

It was, she realized despairingly, as clear a statement of possession to all who were within watching distance as if he'd shouted it from the playing field.

Too late, Meredith felt her face flame. She stiffened. "Stoney," she hissed. "You had no right—"

"I'll call you tonight," he said. Then he turned and was gone, leaving several people looking at her curiously, including Roger and Tess. And Beth, standing just a few feet away. And her parents.

Just a few people, she thought hopelessly. "You want a ride?" she spoke sharply to Roger. "Let's go."

"Well, aren't we the quiet one?" Roger said knowingly after he'd got in the front seat next to Tess.

"He *kissed* you, Mom," Tess added.

Meredith didn't say anything. Roger laughed, too loudly. "So he did, little niece," he said. "So he did."

Chapter Six

That evening Meredith had to go back and work at the shop. She was actually grateful; she was sure she wouldn't be able to sleep tonight anyway.

She still couldn't believe that he'd kissed her, right in front of *everyone*. Deliberately. And he'd known what he was doing: in that single public act, he'd changed irrevocably the rules of the game being played between them. In a small town like Colton, no one would have any trouble interpreting the message he was communicating—he'd branded her his, for all to see.

It was one of the minor miracles of family life that nobody said anything about the kiss at their late, after-game dinner. Roger had gone into one of his irrational moods again; he was sulky and rude. Her mother and father carried on a rather forced conversation about the rounds her father had made at the hospital, thirty miles away. Even Tess was uncustomarily reticent. Her usual chatter was confined to one rather lengthy description of a story the teacher had read that day in school. When she was finished, no one had anything more to say.

Roger had just pushed himself away from the table when the phone rang. They were eating in the kitchen; the phone was on the wall behind his right shoulder. He leaned his chair back and reached for the receiver.

"Hullo? Oh, hi, Coach." There was half a minute of silence before Roger gave Meredith a slow, mocking look. "Yeah. No trouble. She's right here." He put the phone against his chest. "Yours, Merry." He leered, making silent smacking motions with his lips.

Abruptly Meredith stood. "If you don't mind," she said to her family, "I'll take this call in the study."

She was halfway down the hall when she heard her father's deliberately low voice reassuring her mother, "Don't look so worried, Kathleen. Meredith can handle herself. She's not going to do anything foolish."

He's right, Meredith told herself. I can handle Stoney Macreay. Which belief lasted until she heard Stoney's voice.

"When can I see you again?" Stoney asked without introduction. Then he added, "I need to."

She felt a curious, unfamiliar sensation in the pit of her stomach. Her breath caught in her throat; she knew a moment of fear. "I—I don't know whether—"

"When, Meredith?" The impatience in his tone told her he wasn't in the mood to listen to panicked excuses.

She closed her eyes and leaned against the wall. "Friday," she whispered.

The silence on the other end of the phone told her nothing. Then, in a voice curiously devoid of any feeling at all, Stoney said, "Good." He seemed to hesitate. "Good. What time?"

"Eight-thirty. After I get Tess in bed."

"Do you want to go out to dinner?"

"No. I'll eat with my daughter."

"We'll go into Logansport, then," Stoney said. "There's a place there I've been wanting you to see."

"What is it?"

"A surprise. Something special."

"Oh." Her heart was beating like a soldier's drum.

"Meredith?"

"What?"

"Don't chicken out."

"No. I won't."

"Just be waiting for me on Friday, okay?"

"Okay," she said softly.

"Good."

"'Bye, Stoney."

She went back to the kitchen. Everyone was still there, even Roger. "That's a silly expression you're wearing," her brother teased. It was Tess who asked the question that was written on every face. "What did he want, Mom?"

Meredith took a deep breath. She forced a bright, carefree smile. "I'm going out with him," she said evenly. "On Friday night. After Tess is in bed."

"Woo-woo-woo," Roger said.

"Do you think that's wise?" her mother began.

"Mom!" Tess wailed. "I don't want to be in bed! I won't even get to see him! Can't I stay up? Until he gets here?" Then she said, "Wait till I tell all my friends my mom is going out with Coach!"

Good grief. She and Stoney would be fodder for the gossip mills for weeks.

"Of course you can stay up, dear," Meredith's mom answered Tess distractedly.

"Kathleen!" Meredith's dad remonstrated. "You let your daughter set the rules for her own child!"

"Oh, dear." Meredith's mom was immediately repentant. "I didn't mean to contradict—"

"It's okay," Meredith said, trying to lessen the protective tension she felt emanating from her mother. "It's just a date, everyone. Hey. Don't make more out of it than it is. And besides—" she repeated the assurance she'd given herself earlier "—I can handle Stoney Macreay."

"I bet he'd like to handle you," Roger said suggestively.

"Shut up, brat," Meredith said. She looked at her mother and deliberately changed the subject. "Mom, don't worry about the dishes. I'll do them."

Her father scraped his chair back from the table and stood up. "You going back to the shop tonight, Sunshine?" he asked, gathering plates from the table.

Meredith nodded. "Afraid so. Things are really piling up."

"You go on, then," her mother offered. "I'll take care of the kitchen."

"But Tess—"

"I can put her to bed, too."

Meredith looked at her family. Her mother and father, who loved her, she sometimes felt, almost too much. Her little brother, teetering on the very verge of manhood, with all its attendant challenges. Her daughter, who was happily helping her grandpa clear the table. So much peace here, she thought. So much security. How could she ever think of leaving?

And yet to stay was to remain forever a child in her parents' house.

The thought seemed almost traitorous. Impulsively Meredith threw her arms around her mother and gave her a hug. "You're one in a million, Mom, and I love you."

Her mother hugged her back before grasping her arms with surprising strength. "Just remember to be careful," she said fiercely. "With Stoney Macreay."

"I will be," Meredith promised solemnly. "You have my word on it."

The whole family managed to be in the living room when Stoney called for her on Friday night. Even Roger and Beth were there, watching television. It was the first Friday Roger had been home since Meredith could remember, and she had the sneaking suspicion he was only waiting around to see if his coach was really going to show up for a date with his big sister. Meredith hated to admit that she had her doubts, too.

Stoney showed up.

He had dressed with the casual elegance she remembered, in a richly colored dark brown sports coat and incredibly fine-looking tan linen slacks. His cream-colored shirt had tiny yellow lines running through it. His white blond hair was combed back from his head. He looked as he had in the days of his glory, before his knee knocked him out of pro sports for good.

She remembered her promise to her mother. But how can you be careful with a god? she wondered helplessly as she watched Stoney effortlessly charm her family. He talked easily with her parents, joked with Roger, swung Tess up on his shoulder. Tess squealed with delight and then asked, "Do you like my mommy?"

"Yes," Stoney said simply, lifting Tess down before hunkering down himself so that he was the child's size.

"Are you going to marry her?"

Meredith sucked in her breath. Roger barked out a laugh. Meredith's mother's cheeks turned rosy. "Tess," she remonstrated sharply.

Where had Tess come up with a question like that? How would Stoney deal with it?

Easily enough, it seemed. Stoney gave her daughter his low, glamorous smile. "Would you like that?" he asked.

Tess nodded. "I want a daddy," she said.

Stoney's smiled faded. "You wish you had a daddy." His tone was gravely serious.

"Yeah. MaryJane's daddy gives her presents all the time when he comes to visit. Will you bring me presents?"

Stoney's expression changed to one of rueful comprehension. Still, he took a moment to answer, giving the impression he was seriously considering Tess's question. "Your mommy and grandparents give you all the presents you need," he said. "I don't think you need a daddy to do that."

"And someone else," Tess said importantly.

"What?"

"Someone else gives me a present on my birthday. My secret friend."

A smile toyed around the edges of Stoney's mouth. He threw a quick look at Meredith. She acknowledged it with a little inclination of her head.

So, he seemed to be saying. *You let her keep them.* The smile that sprang to Stoney's face was for Meredith alone; she felt her cheeks heat in response to it. Then he turned back to Tess. "That's pretty special, to have a secret friend," he said softly.

"Yes. No one else at school has one. I told all about my secret friend during sharing time one day, and you know what? No one else gets presents from a secret friend like I do."

"I see." Stoney's voice was deliberately light.

"When I was a baby I used to think my friend was my daddy, but I don't think that anymore. A daddy would let you know, wouldn't he? He'd tell you who he was."

This was news to Meredith. She hadn't realized her daughter was fantasizing about the father she never had.

"Hmm," Stoney said.

"I'd like a daddy, actually. Whether he brought me presents or not." Tess's voice was wistful.

Stoney unfolded his long, lean body and stood up. "Maybe some day," he said to Tess gently, "you'll get one." He turned with purposeful intent to Meredith. "Ready to go?"

"Sure."

"When are you going to bring my mommy home?" Tess demanded suddenly.

Stoney looked nonplused. He obviously wasn't used to accounting for his time to a five-year-old child.

Amused, Meredith rescued him. "Grandma's going to put you to bed. We'll be back after you're asleep."

"Maybe I won't be asleep," Tess argued stubbornly.

"I'll stop by your room and check. And I'll kiss you whether you're asleep or not."

That seemed, at last, to meet Tess's needs.

"Have a good time, Meredith," her father said, rising from his easy chair.

"I will, Dad." She kissed her father on his cheek. "Goodbye Mom. Rog."

"Hey, Coach." Roger shifted slightly on the sofa. "What?"

"Don't do anything I wouldn't do."

"You got it." Stoney put a deliberately casual arm around Meredith's waist. "See you at the game tomorrow."

"See you," Roger said.

They weren't halfway down the driveway when Stoney started to laugh. Meredith gave him a confused look.

"I haven't been so thoroughly vetted since I was a kid."

It may have been funny to Stoney, but standing there watching her family give Stoney the once-over had been more than a little embarrassing to Meredith, underscoring as it had the feelings that had been troubling her lately—of still being a child, of being unformed, unseparated. Her discomfort made her speak with unthinking asperity. "They're concerned, Stoney."

Immediately his laughter faded. Meredith felt its loss like a cloud passing over the sun. "I'm probably not their number-one choice for you, huh, Meredith?" he said flatly. "Not that I blame them. I'd probably feel the same way, under the circumstances."

"I'm not sure they know what to think," she answered honestly. "I'm not sure I do, either, actually." When he didn't respond, she turned and looked out the window.

She wished she could think of some small talk. But she couldn't think of anything. Ever since Stoney had called and asked her for this date, she'd been in such a state of uncharacteristic expectation, almost of *joy*. Yet here she was now, tongue-tied and schoolgirl shy, unable to think of anything to say.

She continued to stare out the window, feeling miserably uncertain and insecure, sure that Stoney would soon wish he'd never even asked for this date.

"Meredith."

She turned back to him.

"Don't worry about it. I like your family. I just thought it was a little funny, that's all." He reached out and touched her cheek. "Okay?"

And just as suddenly everything was all right, after all. Her blood was singing again. Her heart was throbbing just as it had a hundred times this week. Her lips curved upward in a smile. "Okay," she agreed happily.

He turned serious. "When you look at me like that, I almost think . . ." He hesitated.

"What?"

"Nothing."

"No, really. What?"

"You won't get mad?"

"I don't know," she said, truthful as ever. "But I want to know what you were thinking."

He moved his hand back to the steering wheel and stared straight ahead. "You look like some damned innocent. You're not very experienced, are you?"

She felt her elation drain out of her. "You can't have a baby and stay innocent, Stoney," she said, stating the obvious.

His hands tightened against the wheel. "No," he agreed grimly. "You can't."

So much for small talk, she thought.

He took her into Logansport, as he'd promised, to a place that was a sort of blend between a nightclub and a coffeehouse. The room was dimly lit; there were small, intimate tables covered with white tablecloths scattered throughout. A single candle burned on each table. A lone musician was playing acoustic guitar at the front of the room. Through a side door Meredith could just glimpse some shelves full of books. "A kind of informal alternative lending library," Stoney explained casually.

That was the point at which she began to relax. She'd assumed that Stoney would be a traditionalist—he'd take her to a show, maybe out for something afterward. She'd thought that sometime during the evening he'd probably manage to display some of his spoils of macho victory—she'd heard he'd developed quite a fortune while he was pro. But never once had she dreamed he'd take her to a place like this.

This place was sophisticated yet intimate. Classily subdued. The kind of place where you went when you wanted to enjoy someone's company and just be yourself.

The room was full but not crowded. People sat singly or in small groups, listening to the music, speaking in low voices to each other. A bearded man wandered in from the library room, an open book in his hand. Stoney took

Meredith's arm and led her to an empty table in a far corner. "I thought this would be a good place to just sit and talk. Get to know each other." He held out her chair, then seated himself at her immediate right. Their knees touched beneath the table.

Meredith felt herself sigh. A waitress came; Stoney ordered some sort of exotic coffee and European dessert cakes for both of them. The musician finished his set and was replaced by a young woman with long straight hair. "Shh," Stoney said when Meredith would have spoken. "Listen."

The young woman began to sing an old ballad; she had the clearest, sweetest contralto voice Meredith had ever heard. Gradually the room grew silent as the song swelled from the woman's throat, her incredible voice wrapping everyone there in the spell of ancient sorrows and all too human grief. Meredith thought that there couldn't be a person in that room who wasn't remembering some troubled time, some loss, some sadness that hadn't quite healed over.

Then that song ended, and the singer tossed her head and moved into something lighter, gayer, the words and tune defying the dark side of life, as if just by singing the woman could direct them all to look toward the light.

"Who is she?" Meredith whispered.

"Leona Mark. An old friend of mine from college," Stoney said. "She settled here with her husband, three years ago. Now that I live close, I come down to hear her whenever I can."

"She's marvelous."

"I thought you'd like her."

Meredith's hands were on the table, circling her coffee cup. Very casually Stoney brought his left hand up to lift one of hers away from the cup. His knee pressed almost imperceptibly closer to hers. He took her hand and laid it on the table in front of him, then covered it with his own. They were silent—both of them listening to that incredible voice. She was intensely conscious of his hand on hers. His fingers played with hers or stroked the back of her palm or simply covered her hand with the warmth of his larger one. Meredith closed her eyes and listened to the music and felt a fire grow inside her, flaming out from the joining of their hands.

Everything else faded away. Her life in Colton, her business, her struggles to break free. Even Tess. There was only this room and this song and the feel of Stoney's hand on hers. And a strangely fluid strength coiling and uncoiling itself in her center, arranging itself in alternating patterns of waiting and wanting, of patience and passion, of fear and desire.

At last Meredith and Stoney began to speak, their voices low, their words coming more easily now. Meredith forgot her wariness. She listened as he talked of coming home to Colton, of trying to find a resting place. Of the boys on his team. Of knowing they could win the state championship, really knowing it. He said it proudly, watching her. But the words were nothing compared to other things. Even after his hand released hers, Stoney touched her—his leg against her knee, his fingers brushing her cheek, her hair, his hand lightly touching her shoulder. And then he took her hand again and put it on his thigh, and laid his atop, his thumb stroking her knuckles, her fingers, her smooth skin. All the while she felt the tightness of corded muscle and deceptive strength.

When Leona Mark was done singing, she came to their table. "Stoney!" she exclaimed. "How wonderful to see you!" She sat down and smiled at Meredith. "Introduce us."

"Meredith Blackmoore, Leona Mark," Stoney said easily.

"How exciting that he's actually brought a *woman*," Leona laughed. "We'd begun to think Stoney had turned into a monk."

Meredith remembered the blonde and eyed Stoney doubtfully. As if reading her thoughts, he gave a rueful grin. "A minor interruption," he said softly. "She came after me. I, however, had someone else in mind."

"Hmm," Leona said in reaction to their lowered voices and private communication. She placed a hand on Stoney's arm. "I can see I'm definitely *de trop* here. Bring her by the house sometime, Stoney. Let her meet the man and the brat."

"I'll do that," Stoney agreed.

"You sing beautifully," Meredith said, leaning forward. "I was spellbound."

A big smile split Leona's face. "For that you can come by anytime, even without Stoney," she offered.

"Thanks," Meredith said, feeling suddenly warmed. "I'll keep it in mind."

They left the coffeehouse a short time later and drove in silence toward home. Stoney was smiling slightly; Meredith knew an odd feeling of peace.

Something had happened tonight—something she was sure was quite marvelously rare. She and Stoney had passed the point of mere desire, and had also become...friends. Stoney stretched his arm out so that his hand curved around her neck. She leaned back, feeling his fingers stroke the bare skin there.

All her old prejudices were melting away; it seemed to her that someone new was emerging—someone she liked, someone she could admire, even, she thought, someone she could trust.

Stoney moved his hand to touch her face. He began to massage her lips with the pad of his thumb.

All thought left her then. Her eyes glazed as her mouth dropped open slightly. Her breathing grew slightly ragged. Her body became somnolent, heavy—yet she felt oddly weightless. Through all these sensations she was again feeling the song of joy she'd felt that other time, when Stoney had kissed her in her shop. Yes, her body seemed to call. Yes, her spirit answered. Yes. Yes. Yes.

She kissed his thumb in near gratitude and heard him groan in response.

She kissed it again.

Yes.

They were almost to Colton when a car suddenly blasted past them, its windows down in spite of the cool autumn air, its radio blaring. Meredith's eyes flew open; Stoney's hand left her face. Both of them looked at the passing car.

Drunken, uninhibited laughter left its briefly shocking imprint on the night air. Then, just for a second someone in the car switched on the interior light.

Meredith sucked in her breath. Fear clutched her heart. She knew that car. She knew those kids. Roger was with them. With Beth.

Stoney swore. "You saw?" he said.

"Roger's in there! With Beth!" She wrapped her arms around her suddenly nauseous stomach. It had been Steven Mines's parents' car—Steven was driving. And she'd seen Brett Blankenship, too. And at least two others.

Steven was one of Stoney's starting forwards; Brett was his star goalie.

Stoney pushed down on the accelerator. His sports car jumped forward.

The speeding vehicle in front of them roared in crazy motion around a curve. Stoney pressed on, trying to catch up. But Steven Mines, obviously sensing a chase, went faster still. His car bounced off the shoulder, spewing up gravel.

Didn't they know it was their coach? Meredith thought. Hadn't someone recognized Stoney's car? But it was night, and those kids weren't noticing anything.

Stoney pressed on.

Steven swung wide on another turn, then overcompensated to the right.

"Don't, Stoney!" Meredith cried in near terror. "Don't chase those kids. They're obviously— Oh, please stop! Look at them! They think it's a game!"

Steven's car was in the middle of the road now, its rear waving dangerously.

"Oh, God," Meredith moaned. "Don't chase them anymore. Please."

Slowly Stoney lifted his foot off his accelerator. Meredith watched the taillights of the speeding car fade away into the distance. She was shaking everywhere.

Stoney eased his car over to the shoulder. He seemed a little pale himself. "Okay," he said to her grimly. "Okay. You're right. They're gone. Maybe they'll even get home safely."

"They were drunk," she said. "You saw them. Drunk or high or both."

"I know, Meredith."

"What are you going to do about it, Stoney? They're in *training*. You're their coach." Her voice had risen sharply; she was in danger of becoming hysterical. But she'd been so scared—was scared still.

"Hey," Stoney said. "I know the rules. I'll talk to them tomorrow, Meredith."

"Will you kick them off the team?"

"We didn't catch them. We won't have any proof."

Meredith closed her eyes. She saw again the interior of that speeding vehicle. Roger had been *laughing*. She saw herself at sixteen. She remembered Tom, drinking, partying. He'd laughed at the rules, too. Nobody had ever stopped him. He'd done what he wanted, just as he said.

Emotion swept her. Anger. Hurt. Fear. Confusion. Guilt. Shame. Loss. As if Tom had hurt her only yesterday, as if all the decisions she'd made as a result of that one night were new and fresh. Only now it was worse, a hundred times more intense.

"Somebody should stop them," she whispered. "Somebody should do something."

She thought of Beth, begging her to keep her secrets. She thought of Roger, laughing as that car drove its death dance down the road. She thought of Tess, growing up in a world that passed its sick madness from generation to generation.

A picture formed itself in her mind—the soccer field during Roger's last game. The fans calling out their relentless cheers, screaming encouragement to their madly scrambling team. "Win!" they screamed. "Score! Come on, heroes! Massacre them!"

"You've got to do more than *talk* with them," she told Stoney tensely. "These guys don't understand talk. They understand action, Stoney."

"Like you said, I'm their coach. I'll handle it."

That's right, she thought bitterly. She understood too well. He had an unbeaten team. State-championship material. He wouldn't want to do anything to endanger that.

"All right. I'll bench them," he snapped, responding to the condemnation in her silence. "Two games. I don't need proof for that."

"It's not enough," she argued. "You need to do more than that."

"Right. I have no real proof that they were doing anything except speeding. So I'll just mosey back onto that road and catch up with them and pull them over. After I do that I'll administer a Breathalyzer and take urine samples." He was catching her mood; his tone was sarcastic.

She turned away from him and stared out the window. "If you did that," she said, deliberately taking his words at face value, "you might forfeit the state championship, huh, Stoney?"

Angry silence answered her. His knuckles tightened against the wheel. Then, very softly he said, "Do I hear an accusation in there somewhere?"

She continued to stare at the night-dark landscape. They weren't very far from town. It was the same scenery she'd known since she was a very small girl. So little changed. So much remained the same.

"Meredith?"

"I hate games," she said.

Again that awful, separating silence.

When she couldn't stand it anymore, she continued rashly. "Especially here, in Colton. Winning is everything. Being the big hero. Being a stud."

"Look," he said coldly. "I tried to catch those kids. You're the one who stopped me."

He was right, of course. It wasn't his fault. Tom wasn't, his father wasn't, this town wasn't.

"Sorry," she said stiffly.

"Meredith. I *am* going to bench those kids."

She turned to him. He looked withdrawn, full of shadows and fierce anger.

"Beth came to see me," she said, trying to explain. "Last Sunday. She told me Roger was drinking and using drugs." She took a deep, shuddering breath. "And I didn't tell anyone. I didn't tell Mom or Dad or anyone. If something happens to him tonight, I'll never forgive myself."

Stoney watched her, saying nothing.

"I know what you're thinking," she said. "That I wasn't so different when I was that age. And maybe I wasn't." She caught her bottom lip in her teeth to keep it from trembling and looked away.

"You were different," Stoney said at last. "It was written all over you. You were young and beautiful and way out of your league." He gave a short bark of laughter. "And you were my brother's, besides. Yet even that didn't seem to matter—"

"No!" she said. "I wasn't Tom's."

"Meredith." His voice was low and somehow sad. "You have Tess. At one time, at least, you were Tom's."

She felt suddenly, violently, ill. She put her head in her hands and leaned over her knees. Say it, a voice inside her ordered. Tell him the truth. But all she could manage was a ragged, whispered denial. "No." Air rushed through her ears. She had the oddest sensation of falling.

Some misery in her expression must have touched Stoney's protective instincts. He reached out and touched her cheek, and the gentleness of it startled her. She raised her head, stared at him and said starkly, "Your brother raped me, Stoney."

It took a moment for his eyes to narrow, for his knuckles to turn white. A low, feral growl came from his throat. "Tom did what?"

Tears pooled behind her eyelashes. She clenched her hands in tight fists in her lap.

"Rape," he repeated flatly.

She nodded jerkily and looked away.

"When?"

"That night. When I met you. Tom was drunk and jealous and—"

"I know what he was. I remember. I remember everything. You looked so damned lost. So damned beautiful and young and lost." Stoney's tone was grimly fierce. "No wonder you didn't want anything to do with me." His eyes were slits of golden fire. "I'll kill him."

"Right." She managed a rough laugh. "Your *brother*. Besides—" she tossed her head "—it was a long time ago. I'm over it completely." Tears coursed down her cheeks.

Stoney reached over the gearshift to cup her face with his hand. "Meredith?"

She looked at him through wounded, grief-drenched eyes.

"I'll make you forget Tom. I'll make you forget he ever existed."

"How can you do that?" she shot back, but already she felt the powerful seduction of his words. "I'll never forget, ever. And there's Tess. I love Tess, but..." Her shoulders started to shake.

"You were too young," he said gently. "You're a fine mother, Meredith Blackmoore, but you were too young."

"Yes," she whispered.

"But you're not too young now. I want to make you mine, Meredith. You and Tess both."

It was too much. She was having trouble thinking straight, so she gave up thinking altogether. She closed her eyes and remembered again how she felt when Stoney kissed her.

The intensity of the emotion that followed terrified her. She was more afraid than she had ever been in her whole life. She tried her best to face it, to face down her fear.

"You're scared, aren't you?"

"No—no, of course not."

"Terrified," he said in a curiously flat voice.

"I—I..." She looked at him blankly. "Yes," she said.

"I'd like you to come home with me. To my place. Tonight."

"Tonight?" Her voice sounded like a squawky whisper.

"Just to talk, Meredith. Just to learn to be...friends. Would you like that?"

At that moment she didn't know. She didn't know anything.

"All right," she heard herself say.

Giving a small smile, Stoney drove the rest of the way to Colton.

Chapter Seven

Stoney let her into his house, brushing her shoulder with his arm as he pushed his door open. She jumped at the contact, and he moved away.

Stoney lived in a spacious two-story, three-bedroom house in the middle of town. His living room was very upscale—white walls, modern earth-tone furniture, brilliantly colored prints of obscure contemporary artists on the walls.

Meredith stood in the middle of the living room, holding her purse, feeling entirely disoriented. What had seemed so right just a moment ago now seemed like a terrible mistake.

Stoney's kitchen was adjacent to the living room. She watched him as he disappeared into it, heard the sound of running water, of a pot being placed on a stove.

Still she stood, not turning or moving in any way.

He appeared in the kitchen doorway, leaning against it easily. "Sit down," he ordered her gently. He made a gesture toward the leather sofa.

She did as he suggested. She discovered she was shaking. She eyed him warily. She clutched her purse against her breast. "I've never told anyone," she said in a low tone. "About Tom. You're the first person I've told. Ever."

Something flickered in the back of his eyes, some spark of warm compassion chased by a look of fierce protectiveness. Then that, too, was gone. His face was carefully expressionless.

She turned from him to gaze blindly at his coffee table. Gradually her eyes focused on the items there—crystal candlesticks and an obviously unread book on a sixteenth-century artist. "This is a cold house," she said softly. "Don't you like caring about where you live, Stoney?"

He froze for an instant, then paced to the large front window and stared out into the street.

She was instantly contrite. "I'm sorry, Stoney. Truly." Inside herself she was sad as a child who had been lost for a long time. She didn't know what she'd expected when she finally spilled her secret, but she knew she hadn't expected this. Yet she wasn't the only one who had secrets. She looked at Stoney—his back was to her now, his hands clenched together behind him, his blond head thrown up, his eyes looking out at the night-darkened sky. She watched him and waited.

"Tom really was a bastard," he said at last with seeming irrelevance. When she didn't respond, he continued. "But he didn't come out of nothing. Do you understand that? Tom ... when he was a kid, he was as gentle and kind a brother as you can imagine."

She didn't know that Tom, could hardly believe he had ever existed. "He changed," she said flatly.

"Yeah." Stoney's gravelly dry tone was painful to hear, it was so full of secret knowledge. "He changed."

"He hurt me."

Abruptly Stoney left his position at the window to seat himself at her side. His face was curiously void of expression. He pulled Meredith into his arms. She felt how tense he was. How...explosive. She put her head on his chest, not saying anything. They stayed that way for several minutes. Not speaking. Not moving. Just holding each other.

"Stoney," she finally said, her voice low and confused. "What are you thinking?"

He started to play with her hair. A shudder went through her as he hand combed it, over and over. "Nothing," he replied.

"Liar."

"Kiss me," he said.

She did, realizing even as she did so that he was stalling deliberately, not answering her question. But it was still wonderful. *He* was wonderful. She marveled anew that this felt so right, so...essential. Stoney Macreay, she thought. Only him. Only he makes me feel this way.

And then her thoughts ceased, as once again she felt herself open up, become soft and pliable and eagerly welcoming. And again the song of life rushed through her: I can! I can! Yes! Yes! Yes!

She felt his hand brush her cheek, her hair. It moved down, to her neck, the curve of her breast, her waist. His mouth shifted, slanted, and she opened beneath it, gasping and laughing and crying his name.

Joy.

She would offer him everything, deny him nothing.

"Meredith," he murmured. "Meredith." Her name on his lips was a hymn of life. Please, she thought. I never thought I could feel like this, please, please, please don' stop now. I don't care who you are or what you've been or who've you've been with. I don't care don't care don' care....

It took her a long time to understand he was actually telling her something. "Meredith. We've got to stop, Merry. Before we lose control, honey. Meredith."

She didn't want to stop.

"Meredith." He shook her a little. She opened her eyes and stared at him. He had a lean and hungry look, his eyes dark and flaming, his nostrils flaring, his mouth swollen and bruised slightly—like hers must be. His very small but still crooked smile was almost wry.

"Stoney?" she said.

"You are so beautiful. So innocent."

She took a deep, disbelieving, shuddering breath. She felt a rush as if a windstorm were moving through her. Thoughts swirled and ebbed in sudden confusion through her brain. She thought of Tess, bright and pure and young. Having a father now, if what Stoney was offering was true.

She thought about college and her lost dreams. Profound pain filled her breast as repressed longings exploded within her.

Then she was sixteen again, and saw Tom's laughing, leering face, smelled his drunken breath as he kissed her. *Take me home, Tom,* she heard herself plead. But he hadn't taken her home and—

Now she was back in the present, feeling Stoney's arms around her, so comforting and warm. She could sleep there and be safe. Wonderingly she reached up and touched his cheek.

"I want you, Meredith. So much." His voice was raggedly hoarse.

It was then she had the strangest reaction of all. She cried.

Suddenly, with terrible unexpectedness, the tears burst from her eyes and rolled down her cheeks. Noisily, messily they came, forcing her to breathe with great gasping gulps.

Stoney shot upright. "Meredith?" He wrapped his arms around her and patted her helplessly. "Don't cry, honey," he said. But through it all she felt something else in him, some anger, and after a while he said, with quiet bitter resignation, "Forget I mentioned it, then."

She tried to stop, to tell him not to worry, that her tears weren't his fault, but so great was her release she could hardly speak, hardly breathe. After a very long time she managed to calm herself a little. Stoney said stiffly, "I'll take you home now."

"No!" she said, twisting in his arms, realizing she had to say something—anything—to explain her outburst. "I bet you've never had that reaction before," she managed to say with a jerky laugh.

A dull red stained his cheeks.

"I've never felt this way, Stoney," she admitted in a low, husky tone. "But...you hardly know me." Then she amended, "We don't know each other."

After a long moment he said, his voice even and low, "Sure. All right. So let's get acquainted. Tell me about you."

"There's nothing to tell."

"One thing," he commanded. "Tell me one important memory."

She took a still-shaking breath. She could manage that. A memory came to her, pure and vivid as if it had happened only yesterday.

"All right," she agreed. "I'll do it."

He settled her in his arms so that her head was leaning against his shoulder. His arms encircled her. "I'm listening," he encouraged her.

"One morning when I was eight years old, my father came in late from surgery. He's always kept unusual hours, just like most doctors do. He'd been out all night—something we were pretty well used to. I'd just gotten up. I was headed toward the kitchen seeking breakfast when I heard him and my mother in our living room. He was still dressed in his work suit—my mother had on a long, flowing purple robe. I'll always remember the color of that robe, Stoney. Because my dad was kneeling by her chair, weeping into my mother's lap. She was leaning over him, rubbing his back, kissing his head.

"'What's wrong?' I asked, alarmed. I'd never seen my father cry before.

"'Mark Allen was in an accident last night,' my mother said.

"'Mark Allen?' Mark was my first puppy love—his parents and mine were best friends. I idolized him—he seemed so vibrant, so grown-up and...alive. He'd just gotten his license the week before, and he'd promised to take me driving. 'What happened?' I whispered. 'He's all right, isn't he?'

"My mother shook her head. 'Your daddy tried all night to save him...'

"I could barely comprehend what she was saying. I watched, stunned, as my mother put her arms around my dad and rocked him, crooning to him like he was a child. Roger came into the room, wanting Mother. I picked him up and held him and crooned to him, just like my mother was doing to my dad.

"Mark Allen is dead, I thought. Daddy couldn't save him. Mark Allen is dead.

"Eventually my mother talked my father into having some toast. She had just gone to prepare it when the doorbell rang. My dad was sitting exhausted in his chair by this time, so I answered the door.

"There was a woman standing there I'd never seen before. I remember thinking she wasn't dressed very well—she looked old and plain. And she looked...desperate. She was hugely pregnant, and she was gasping slightly. She asked for my father, calling him Dr. Blackmoore.

"My dad was right there, of course. He got to his feet and came over. She was going to have a baby, she said. Right away. But she was afraid to go to the hospital because she didn't have any money or any way to pay. She knew my dad because of some volunteer work he did at the local clinic. Could he do something? Call the hospital or something?

"I peeked around my father and saw an old beat-up car parked in our driveway, with a man at the wheel, looking terribly tense, smoking a cigarette. My dad asked the woman how soon she was going to have the baby, and she said she'd been having pains all night. It must have been hard for her to talk, because her breathing became louder. Suddenly her eyes got kind of wild, and she took a couple of steps in and crumpled up on our living room floor. My dad knelt down beside her and felt her pulse, and then she gave a low scream, and suddenly the floor was all wet with water and blood. My father shouted to my mother to call for an ambulance. Then the man from the car was inside our house, holding the woman's hand. My dad turned the woman over on her side and pulled her skirt up to her waist. He'd totally forgotten me—I was still standing there holding Roger.

"'You're having this baby right now!' he told her. 'You'd better push hard!'

"She closed her eyes and moaned, just once. Her face got really red. And then the baby was there, sliding right out of her body. I remember being totally amazed—that this was how babies are born. And its eyes, it had the clearest blue eyes. That baby blinked and looked at all of us in that room. To this day I think she even smiled.

"My mother came running in with a towel and some hot water and saw me there. For a minute she looked startled, and I thought for sure she would send me away, but instead she told me to come over and look at this new baby. My dad was still holding it in his hands. His face was so tired, and he was kneeling over this strange, half-naked woman, but there was something about him—something so luminous and radiant that nothing else seemed to matter. He showed the baby to the man who'd come in and then to my mother and then to me.

"'She's beautiful,' my mother said. The man kept apologizing, but the whole time he was grinning from ear to ear. My mother got a pillow and blanket for the woman, and helped my father lift her out of her dress, and they laid the baby on the woman's breast. Then the ambulance was there. Some men came in and laid the woman and her baby on the stretcher and took her away. They never cut the umbilical cord or anything. I remember thinking how connected they were. And the woman looked so peaceful—her eyes were closed and her hand kept stroking her baby's body.

"My father looked at the carpeting on the living room floor. 'Guess we'll have to get you a new rug,' he told my mother. But neither one of them seemed angry or anything. I went up to my dad, and he put his arm around me and Roger. 'You just saw a miracle, Sunshine,' he said. Then he added, so soft I could barely hear, 'You just saw why I love being a doctor.'

"'Even though sometimes people die?' I asked.

"'Even though,' he agreed. And right then, staring at the bloody wet spot on our living room rug, and remembering that newborn baby looking around at us with all the awe of a faraway traveler in her eyes, I knew I wanted to be a doctor. I wanted to do what my father did. He'd spent all night working to save a life. Even though he failed, he still had the strength to help bring a new one into the world. He became a kind of hero to me then, a life-giver, and I wanted to become just like him."

At last Meredith was silent. Stoney was still holding her, stroking her arm. He didn't say anything, but she sensed he wasn't angry anymore. She felt him plant a kiss on her head.

"I gave up that dream for a long time, Stoney," she said quietly. "I don't think I can give it up again."

She wanted him to say something encouraging, but all he said was, "I understand," and his tone was hard and flat. Which was how she knew he was still hurting—that in some way *she* was hurting him.

She remembered how he'd kissed her when she'd asked him to reveal *his* thoughts. That kiss had been camouflage. Denial. Stoney obviously wasn't a man used to dissembling.

"What about you?" she challenged. "What about your dreams? Did you always want to be a soccer player? What will you do now that your knee is bad? Will you continue to coach for a while?"

She thought at first his harsh laugh was going to be her only answer. She felt him clutch her closer. "Stoney," she urged gently. "Your turn. Tell me." Finally she felt a great sigh move through him, and she knew he was preparing to speak.

"How much did Tom tell you? About our family?" Stoney asked.

"Not much. We never got that far, actually."

"So you don't know about Barbara?"

"No."

His voice was low, almost a whisper. She had to strain to hear it. "She's my older sister."

"Older?" Meredith asked. "I thought you were the oldest."

"That's what my dad tells everyone. And that's what my dad told *us* to tell everyone. But it isn't true. Just another Macreay lie to add to all the rest."

He paused, and after a while she realized he really wasn't planning on saying anything else. "Stoney," she said. "Don't stop now."

His hand continued its up-and-down motion on her arm.

"I told you my secret," she said almost fiercely.

He laughed again, this time low and mocking.

"Tell me," she said. She reached out to stop his hand upon her arm, entwining their fingers together.

"I really want to," he said. "Do you know that? I really want to, Meredith."

"Do it, then," she said.

He took a deep breath. His voice dropped to a near monotone. "There were five of us—two girls and three boys. I was the second born. Barbara came first. Then Tom. The other two—Billy and Clarissa—were years younger. So that Tom and Barbara and I formed sort of a separate family.

"To this day I can remember Barbara's smile, though in later years we hardly saw it. She was made to be happy, I think. She always saw the best in everybody."

When he paused again, Meredith asked, "How much older than you was she?"

"Two years," he said. "But it might as well have been ten. She was a little mother, really. When we were younger she was always looking out for me, taking care of me."

Meredith understood that; until recently she'd been that way with Roger.

"She understood before I did which way the wind blew, I think. When my dad would enter a room, she'd take me out of it. Though I didn't understand, not at first.

"My dad always enjoyed his beer. But as we got older, it became, for him, more than enjoyment. He drank more and more. For a while I hardly noticed—he didn't pay attention to me, and I didn't pay attention to him. But Barbara started to get all quiet, all . . . inside herself. And later I began to understand more. About where

Barbara's bruises came from. About why she began to always look so frightened. Because when my dad drank, he'd get mean. Little things would set him off. Irrational things. But Barbara protected me. She taught me to watch out for him, stay out of his way. But for some reason she never could. Somehow she caught it more than anybody. In my dad's eyes she couldn't do anything right—he criticized the way she dressed, the way she wore her hair, even her smile. It got to the point he would treat her that way even when he was sober. So she quit smiling. But it didn't help. Whenever he felt violent, Barbara got it.''

"Stoney," Meredith murmured consolingly as she realized anew the enormous difference in their childhoods. How had Stoney lived in a family like that?

"Then my dad started to become more universal. Sometimes he would go after me or one of the other kids. But mostly it was Barbara. In fact, she deliberately deflected his anger toward herself when she could. I couldn't stand it, Meredith—I felt so damned helpless. I was such a helpless, frightened kid. And all the time Barbara was trying to protect me, protect us all.''

Stoney fell silent, remembering. Meredith hardly knew what to say. She brought his hand up and kissed his fingers.

Such a fine hand, she thought with sudden irrelevance. Long and neat and strong.

"But one thing happened that my dad couldn't control. As the years passed, I got bigger. One day I came home from school and my dad was really laying into Barbara. He was holding her by one arm and slapping her face—first on one side, then the other. Over and over again. Her eyes were all glazed and her mouth was bleeding. My mom was standing there crying, and Tom was there, with Billy and Clarissa. They were just standing there, watching their big sister being brutalized in front of their eyes. And then something happened to me. I came unglued, I think. I started screaming and ran right at my dad. He didn't even see me coming. I swung at him with all the strength I had. I can still remember how it felt—my fist connecting with his head. I knocked him out with a single blow. And I was glad, Meredith, *glad*. My mother stopped crying. She came over to me and hugged me and told me she was proud of me and that was the first time in my life I can remember feeling like a hero.''

"How old were you?" Meredith asked softly.

"Thirteen."

Meredith glanced up. Stoney's beautiful face was a portrait of pain and denial. He was staring away from her, his features controlled, tight, as if carved from some ancient stone.

"The strange thing was, when my dad came to, he didn't even seem to mind what I'd done. I'd earned his respect, I guess. After that, if he was mad, he'd always yell at one of my sisters, or at Tom, or even little Billy, or my mom. But never at me. And he never hit me again.

"There was even a period of weeks when he didn't hit anybody else, either. He wouldn't start drinking until he was sure I was going to be home. It was as if he depended on me to keep him from doing his worst.

"Things went along for some time. Then one day Barbara came home from this job she had and came into my room to talk to me. She sat on my bed and held my hand and told me she'd been to see a doctor that afternoon. She was pregnant. And she was terrified, literally scared to death to tell Dad. Her whole body was shaking with fear. I had just turned fourteen—I hardly knew what to do myself. But I promised her I would take care of her, no matter what. Just like she'd always taken care of me.

"Both of us knew it was no use asking Mom for help. Neither Barbara nor I could remember a time when Mom had actually stood up to my dad. If we asked her to break the news for us, she would only suffer for it. And we doubted she would act independently to protect Barbara—she'd never done a thing like that before. That had become my job, you know. The family protector." Stoney made the words into a self-deprecating sneer. "So we waited for a night when my dad seemed almost sober, and then the two of us went in together and told him Barbara was pregnant.

"Only he wasn't as sober as we thought. Within seconds he was totally enraged. He called Barbara names—some of the words he used I'd never even heard before. Then he stood up, grabbed Barbara with his left hand, made a fist with his right and pulled his arm back. I jumped forward, pushed Barbara out of the way and took that blow myself. It was my first black eye, though I hardly felt it at the time. I remember I started shouting at my dad. Told him he was just a drunk—a useless, rotten, terrible old drunk. He looked at me wildly, then sank down onto the floor and started to cry. He curled up in a ball on the floor and blubbered like a baby. It scared Tom, who'd come into the room. I remember Tom staring at me, telling me it was all my fault, screaming at me to leave our daddy alone. And Barbara looked like a miniature version of my mother—all washed out and pinched and afraid. I couldn't remember the last time she'd looked really happy. But then she seemed to straighten up.

"'I'm leaving, Stoney,' she said. 'I'm not staying here any longer.'

"She did leave, that very night. One of her friends came and got her, and we never heard from her for months and months. Finally one day she called the house and talked to Mom and me. She'd gone to a home for unwed mothers, she said. She'd had her baby and given it away. But if she would've kept it, she told me, she would have named it Stoney." He paused and stared into space. When he spoke again, his voice was a mere whisper of sound in the darkened room. "After me."

Meredith was quiet. She was beginning to understand why Tess was so important to Stoney. Tess was his niece, would always be his niece, no matter what the legal documents said. Just as he had a nephew somewhere who in another time and in other circumstances would have borne his name.

After a while she asked, "What happened to Barbara?"

"I don't know. She called me a couple of times after that, but she never came home. I don't know where she is or if she's happy or anything. She just disappeared."

"You blame yourself for that."

He shook his head. "Maybe I do. I promised her, after all—I told her I would take care of her. I would keep her safe."

"You were fourteen."

"Yeah," Stoney said. "I understand now. Or so I tell myself. There was no way, was there?"

"No," Meredith said slowly. "Just like me, you were too young."

They sat for a moment in a kind of drained limbo, a strange sort of peace. The only sounds in the room were made by their mutual breathing. Their bodies were held within each other's arms. Like children, Meredith thought bemusedly. Holding off the world by holding on to each other. Finally she asked, "And you? What happened to you?"

Stoney gave that little self-deprecating shrug she had seen before. "I was just going into high school. It was the first year Colton had a soccer team, and I joined on. It seemed I had a natural affinity for the sport. By the end of the year I was already playing first-string. My dad would come to every game, and somehow my being so good at it seemed to heal him some, too. He drank a little less, for a while. He controlled his temper a little more. By the time he got worse again, I was already a Colton star, and my mom and sisters seemed so proud of me. But Tom—Tom and I were never really friends again.''

''He was jealous.''

''Maybe. Maybe he was confused. It's strange, growing up in a family like that. He became my dad's biggest defender. In Tom's eyes, Dad could do no wrong.

''And I wasn't much of a big brother. After Barbara left, I stayed away from my family as much as I could. I just kept playing soccer. Kept winning. Got a college scholarship. Had offers from the pros. Led the fast life. Tried not to think much about things. Until one day I came home from college and met this girl my brother was dating.'' Stoney's arm tightened around her shoulder. ''She looked so cool, so very lovely. She was young, but it was obvious she was going to be beautiful. Hell, she was already beautiful. She wanted to be a doctor, of all things.'' He wasn't looking at Meredith. ''You were just a kid, Meredith. But I wanted you even then.''

Another time she would think about those words and cherish them. Now there was something else she needed to acknowledge.

''Tom knew you were attracted,'' Meredith said slowly. ''That's probably why he . . . why that night he . . .''

Stoney tilted her face up to him. ''Yes,'' he said, naked understanding in his eyes. Then he said, ''I'm sorry, Merry.''

Maybe now the most important memory of that night should be the one she had suppressed the hardest—how she had felt when she had danced with Stoney, when even though they were strangers and her world had just been ripped apart, she had still felt so incredibly safe and warm in his arms.

She felt safe now.

She looked at him with absolute trust and smiled slowly and sweetly.

He made a groaning sound deep in his throat. He leaned down and kissed her fleetingly on her forehead.

She shook her head, telling him it wasn't enough, that she still wanted more. Only now she understood that he needed loving just as much as she did, and the knowledge was sweet, potent power pouring through her.

He closed his eyes against whatever he saw on her face. "I want to see where this goes, Meredith. I want to get to know you and your daughter. I want to be a part of your life."

They were the wrong words with which to woo her. "Tess isn't part of this. She has nothing to do with us."

"Wrong," he said. "Anyone who is a part of you is also a part of us."

Us. No matter how Stoney made her feel, there really was no *us.* She shook her head to negate his words.

But he brought his head down, so that when she moved, his lips claimed hers.

He gave a growl of desire. His mouth against hers was hot and knowing, filled with hunger and power. Then he seemed to change, grow more controlled. With slow, cool deliberation, he trailed his lips down her cheek to her neck, and then his hand was pushing aside her blouse and his mouth was against the tender skin of her shoulder. "You belong here, with me," he said.

For some reason she wanted to argue with him, to rail against his sensual logic. But the touch and feel and smell of him stopped her, and she was kissing him back, touching him back.

"I'll take care of you, Merry. I'll take care of you and Tess."

Then, in spite of how she felt, of how he felt, so close and fevered against her own hot skin, she heard herself say, softly at first, "No."

"Yes," he murmured against her mouth.

"No," she said more loudly, even though a great, growing hunger, stronger than anything she'd ever known, was rising in her. She pulled her head from his and let him see the determination in her eyes.

"I take care of Tess," she said.

His eyes grew dark. "For now," he said. Then he kissed her one more time, hard and possessive, and she felt it like a brand searing her lips.

She couldn't sleep, of course. Stoney had brought her home hours ago, but she was still wide-awake. She tossed and turned and punched her pillow and totally destroyed the organization of her blankets and sheets. Finally she turned on her lamp and read. At four in the morning she heard the back door open and close.

Roger.

She got out of bed and met him by his bedroom door. He looked wide-eyed and pale. She could smell alcohol on his breath. "What are you doing?" she snapped. "You have to play a game later today."

"Nothing. I'm doing nothing," he slurred.

"You're drunk," she accused angrily.

He shook his head dizzily. "Not me. I only had a couple. I'm fine."

"A couple?" she said in disbelieving outrage. "And you're doing *nothing?* What if Mom and Dad find out? Coach Macreay already knows, you fool. That was his car you guys flew by earlier. And I was in it."

He looked at her. His expression turned from drunken belligerence to drunken horror. "Coach?" he said.

"Coach. As in Stoney Macreay."

He stared at her, aghast.

Meredith continued relentlessly. "And how do you think Mom and Dad will feel when I tell them—"

He grabbed her arm with surprising strength. "No! Don't tell them! Please. I'll quit. This will be it, I promise. No more after tonight." He raised a hand as if he was being sworn in. "I *promise,* Meredith."

Meredith shook her head in disgust.

"Now *you* promise me, Meredith."

"No promises," she said. "I'll think about it."

"Thanks, Merry. Thanks very much. I'll pay you back, you'll see."

"Did you hear me? I didn't promise. I don't ever want you to do this again."

"Right," he said, nodding vigorously. "Never again."

She left him and headed back to bed. She remembered Mark Allen, dead so many years ago, at such a young age. She thought of Stoney's sister Barbara, and her lost child. She thought of Roger, being so damned stupid that he didn't even know he'd risked his life tonight.

And through it all was Stoney, offering her what she'd never thought possible. He could teach her to be a woman. He could teach her everything.

On her way to her room, she looked in on Tess. Her daughter was sleeping peacefully, one arm thrown around her favorite teddy bear.

In spite of what Stoney had said, Meredith knew she wasn't innocent. Tess was the innocent one.

Suddenly, in the midst of her hunger and fear and irrational, unsteady happiness, she had the strongest wish that the whole world could be like Tess. Like Adam and Eve before the Fall, sweet and undefiled, she thought. But she and Stoney weren't innocent, and in that ancient tale, life after knowledge was fraught with pain and peril.

She closed her mind to the thought.

And she would remember again what it felt like to be kissed by Stoney Macreay.

Chapter Eight

Meredith's life was quickly becoming more complex. The next day Colton had an out-of-town soccer game. Stoney called her at work in the morning to tell her he'd reserved a seat for her on the spectator bus.

Immediately Meredith had a sense of free-falling. Stoney was moving fast—purposely assuming she'd agreed to more than she had. She took a deep breath and found herself wishing she could go.

Instead, she said truthfully, "I already told Roger I couldn't be there today. I've got payroll taxes due and billings to get out."

He didn't try to hide his disappointment. "I wanted you there," he said simply. Her face heated until she heard Stoney's next words. "I'm going to bench those boys, and I wanted to have at least one friendly face in the stands." Ah, she thought. Today it's only a friend he wants. Unfortunately, though, she understood all too well what Stoney meant. Colton was a town that liked to win; star players on the bench rarely met that goal.

"You'll do fine," she said sincerely.

"That's no longer possible to do—" Stoney's voice deepened "—without you."

Her heart accelerated in earnest then, and she found herself momentarily speechless.

"I couldn't sleep last night, thinking about you," he continued.

She didn't know what to say, so she was silent, remembering her own sleeplessness.

"I know it's not easy for you to trust, Meredith. But I accept that challenge. I want to teach you to trust me."

"Why?" she asked baldly.

"Because you're a fantastic kisser." There was laughter in his voice now, low and subtly triumphant.

She knew she blushed brightly. Incredible emotion washed over her. She had never felt so desirable or so wanted.

Or so terrified.

"If you can't be at the game, can I see you tonight? Afterward? It'll be late, but I promise I won't keep you too long. I just want to see you."

Suddenly she started talking, too quickly, too brightly. But she didn't want him to sense her fear or her longing. "I don't think so, Stoney. I've had too many late nights this week. And I have so much to do. I'm sorry I won't be at the game, though. I'd like to have been there to support your action in benching Roger and the other guys. You're likely to get some negative responses."

"I can handle negative responses from the fans—"

"Well, I'm sure you can, but . . ."

"Merry. Sweetheart."

There was a strangeness to the word that stopped her in midspeech. *Sweetheart.* She didn't even care if she heard the tiny heartfelt sigh that escaped her lips.

Until the panic reasserted itself.

Stoney was beginning to sound like a serious...
boyfriend. In her mind's eye, she could see exactly where
this would lead. He'd want to take her out, as he'd done
the other night. He'd already kissed her in public.

Colton was a small town. The people in town... the
people would remember who she claimed Tess's father to
be, and the gossip would begin.

It would all be incredibly difficult, especially when she
was still uncertain about some things.

"I'm not your sweetheart," she said. But what she
meant to say firmly instead sounded small and low and
unbelievably sad.

"I'll make you so," he said. "I'll win you yet, Meredith."

"This is not a game," she retorted sharply. "I'm not
a prize to be won, Stoney."

"Did I say that?"

"Yes."

"I didn't mean it so literally."

"All right." She was unconvinced.

"If I can't see you tonight, how about bringing Tess
over to my house for dinner tomorrow?"

He was turning her life upside down. Like the kids'
speeding car the other night, she was spinning crazily,
careening out of control.

"Tess would like that," Meredith said slowly.

"About six?"

"Fine," Meredith said, out of breath now, as if she'd
been running. "We'll be there."

Rumors fly fast and furious in a small town. Meredith
knew what had happened at the game long before Stoney
himself could tell her. Pete Michaels mentioned it when
he came in to order shirts and hats for his sport shop late
that afternoon.

"Heard Macreay got some of our kids benched at the game this afternoon," he said importantly, looking at Meredith with brightly curious eyes. It was obvious he thought she would know something. Stoney's all-too-public kiss had had its effect.

"Is that so?"

"Heard one of them was your brother."

"That's between him and the coach, I guess."

"Macreay's got some people pretty upset, benching Blankenship and Mines like that. First-stringers, including our star goalie."

"I'm sure Coach Macreay had reason," Meredith said calmly.

Pete wasn't the only one who mentioned the benching. Meredith heard the news two more times before the day's end. She heard that at least one of the parents, Brett Blankenship's dad, was furious.

Then, shortly before closing, her mother called. Meredith knew her mother had not been feeling well and had not planned on attending this afternoon's game. "Linda Mines just called. Did you know Stoney was going to bench Roger?"

"He told me he was, Mom."

"Do you think Roger deserved it?"

"Yes. Stoney and I saw him driving around with the others last night. They were going dangerously fast."

"Linda says that everyone is saying those kids were drinking. But I'm sure Roger wouldn't do anything like that."

What could she say? Far be it from her to shatter her mother's universe. Yet she couldn't refrain from saying something. "I think it's a definite possibility, Mom," she said gently.

She could almost see her mother shaking her head on the other end of the phone line. "That's what your father said. But I just can't believe it, Meredith. Roger's not like that. He's never been in trouble or anything."

"It's the way of the world, Mom. Kids party."

"But not Roger," her mother said determinedly. "Not my boy."

When Meredith got home from the shop—well after dinnertime—Tess met her at the door. "Roger's in trouble," she said importantly. "Coach benched him."

Meredith was only halfway through the living room when Roger came storming out of her father's study. His face was red and sullen. He barely glanced at her as he pounded up the stairs with angry feet.

She found her father sitting at his desk, his bowed head cupped in his hands. "Dad?" she said tentatively.

Hudson raised his head. His face looked weary. "Sit down, Meredith."

She did so, in a chair to his immediate right.

"Is Roger into things . . . he shouldn't be?" her father asked.

She shrugged uneasily. "Maybe."

"He swears he's not."

"Oh."

"Have you ever seen him drinking?"

"No," she answered truthfully. But again she found she couldn't be Roger's coconspirator. "But I know he has, Dad."

"Was he drinking last night?"

"Yes."

"You know this? You're not just guessing?"

"I'm not guessing, Dad."

"Ah."

"What will you do?"

"I don't know. I need to talk with your mother. Ground him, I suppose."

"That's good."

Her father gave a little nod. "It's hard being a father, Merry."

"I know, Dad. But you're the best."

He smiled a little. "Thanks, Sunshine."

She stood, leaned over and kissed her father on his nose. "Tomorrow Tess and I are going over to Stoney's for dinner, Dad."

The worry lines deepened on his forehead. "Seeing a lot of Stoney lately, aren't you?"

"Some."

"Know what you're doing?"

"I think so."

"Be careful, Sunshine," her father said. "Though he's a good man, I think."

"I'll be careful, Dad."

But how could she be careful when eyes the color of a storm blazed into hers, the hungry light of possession burning deep within their depths? How could she be cautious when a strong masculine arm surrounded her shoulders, and lips more beautiful than any man's had the right to be brushed hers only lightly, because Tess was there. But she knew he wanted more than that light kiss, and so, God help her, did she. And caution was overwhelmed as he found excuses all evening long to touch her, so innocently, on her neck, her back, her face and once—when Tess wasn't looking—with a carefully deliberate movement across one of her breasts.

It was as if she were in the middle of the ocean, thrown overboard from whatever safe vessel she'd been riding. It was much too late to be careful now. Now was the time to keep her head above water and think merely of survival. Only, unlike the ocean, this eddying current was one of thick delight, and the sweet, potent torment of promised pleasure was the force that drew her down, sucked her in.

Tess was oblivious, thankfully. She was in her own heaven, being in Coach Macreay's home. The first few minutes of the evening she acted like a miniature princess, sitting with precocious dignity in her clean jeans and bright yellow button-down blouse on Stoney's modern sofa.

But it wasn't long before the effort of being dignified gave way to spontaneous childish pleasure. "Gee, Coach, this is a neat house," she said. She leafed through the book on the Grand Canyon. "Have you ever been here?" she asked.

"No," Stoney answered.

"I'd like to go. We learned about it in school."

"Maybe someday we can go together," Stoney suggested.

"Together?"

"You and your mom and me."

Tess's eyes grew wide at that. "Wow!" she breathed. "Really?"

"Stoney..." Meredith began warningly.

He shrugged carelessly. "Anything's possible," he said. But his warm expression belied his neutral words. He smiled at Meredith. "Have I told you yet that you look stunning tonight?"

Meredith was wearing black crepe pants that had grown loose over the past few months, with a simply tailored red shirt on top. She'd pulled her hair back with a plain red-and-black band. She had purposefully underdressed, for reasons she didn't care to think about. Stoney's compliment caught her off guard, so that she couldn't hide her sudden flush of pleasure.

"How about me?" Tess demanded. Meredith's daughter did a little twirl in front of Stoney, her lithe arms outstretched.

"And you are...magnificent," Stoney pronounced seriously.

Tess smiled broadly. Her eyes shining, she turned two more circles before subsiding with a graceful swoosh back onto Stoney's sofa. "Magnificent," she repeated to herself softly. "Magnificent."

Meredith's heart was in her throat. With a single word Stoney had enlarged her daughter's world. Wordlessly she left her own safe haven of Stoney's easy chair to cross the room to where he was leaning against his mantel. She slipped an arm around his waist and kissed him lightly on his cheek. "Thank you," she whispered.

In quick, possessive response his arm snaked out to circle her shoulders, pulling her tight and hard against his body. She felt his face against her hair before he released her. "Hungry?" he asked.

She felt there was no way she could eat a thing, but she nodded anyway. "Sure," she said, her voice husky.

"I'm starving!" Tess announced.

He fed them a surprisingly good Caesar salad, followed by marinated steaks fried with fresh mushrooms, green peppers and tomatoes. When Tess eyed this attractively arranged dish doubtfully, Stoney quickly fried her up a hamburger.

For dessert he offered them gourmet ice cream with fresh blueberries.

As they sat, replete and satisfied, Stoney reached across the table with both hands. With his left he grasped Tess's hand; with his right he took Meredith's. "Let's go for a walk," he suggested.

And that's how they did it, both Meredith and her daughter holding one of Stoney's hands. Only after they'd gone a block or so, Stoney dropped Meredith's hand and wrapped his arm around her shoulder, once again pulling her close.

It was a gorgeous night. The air was incredibly crisp and clean. Birds sang their full-throated evening serenades. They passed children playing in their own front

yards; other youngsters rode their bicycles and in-line
skates on the sidewalks and in the streets. Tess knew several of the children—they exchanged greetings as Tess
proudly held tightly to Coach Macreay's hand.

They saw other people besides children. From her place
on her porch swing, the elderly widow Spinoza waved at
them as they walked by. Mike Callahan, the athletic director of Colton High, lived on this street. He was out
mowing his lawn. When he saw them walking together,
his eyes narrowed before he grinned broadly.

While a part of her despaired at this impossible public
announcement, Meredith had neither the heart nor the
desire to do anything except walk with Stoney Macreay
on this fine autumn night. A strange sort of invasive
happiness was creeping through her. Stoney was right,
though—she did find it hard to trust anything, even her
own feelings. Surely this happiness was to be trusted the
least of all.

Though just for the moment she would accept this
marvelous sense of expectant contentment, enjoy it, not
question it. Yet.

She would save the questions for tomorrow.

This night was hers.

By the time they got back to Stoney's house, dusk had
fallen. Stoney pulled out a Monopoly board, and Stoney,
Meredith and Tess played a noncompetitive game that
had Tess, in spite of her excitement, drooping visibly.
"I'd better take her home," Meredith said.

"No." Stoney replied. "I'd like you to stay for a while.
I'll find an extra blanket, and you can lay her on the
sofa."

Tess offered no objection when Meredith moved her to
Stoney's sofa and covered her with the blanket Stoney
brought. Within minutes Meredith's daughter was asleep.
In the meantime, Stoney built a small fire in the fire-

place; he gathered the extra throw pillows from his furniture and scattered them in front of the fire. He lowered his body so that his back was against his easy chair. With a movement of his arm, he invited Meredith to sit next to him in front of the fire.

Feeling slightly breathless, she did as he asked. Immediately Stoney put his arm around her shoulders and pulled her tight against his body. The only sounds in the room were made by the burning of the small fire and the breeze-blown rustle of Stoney's white venetian blinds. Meredith allowed herself a very small sigh.

"Mmm," Stoney said. "You feel good."

He was right, she thought. She felt good all over. She shifted slightly, so that her head was cushioned more comfortably against his shoulder.

The silence was warm and comfortable. A rare peace seemed to settle around them. The fire burned to embers. Stoney had left only one lamp burning low in a far corner of the room. Everything became peace, comfort and shadows.

In that warm, silent place, with their bodies touching but not yet demanding, trust planted a seed and began to grow.

"Stoney?"

"Hmm?"

"Why'd you come back to Colton?"

His free hand began an up-and-down movement on her arm. She closed her eyes with pleasure. By the time he answered, she had almost forgotten her question.

"A number of reasons, I think," he said, his voice low. "None of them too well thought out. Callahan and I were old friends. When he called and asked me to be soccer coach of Colton High, I thought he was joking. When I realized he was serious, I thought, why not? I wanted a year out, away from the big games and bright lights and too beautiful people, you know? My knee needed to heal.

I needed to think things over. Colton seemed the perfect vehicle.''

It wasn't exactly the answer she'd expected; it wasn't an answer she wholly believed. "Has it done for you what you wanted?" she asked.

"I'm not sure. I think the opposite, actually. It's torn me all up, remembering growing up here. And the boys on the team—they're too much like I was. Only they're at the beginning of their lives, and I'm—I'm finished, Meredith.''

The naked bitterness in his tone wrenched at her heart.

"Hardly finished." She laughed softly. "You still move like a god, Stoney.''

He leaned over her and kissed her hard. "You are so good for me," he said. A rush of feeling swept over her. She wanted that, she thought. She wanted to be good for him. She kissed him back.

He made a deeply masculine sound in the back of his throat. When he raised his head, his eyes were glittering with a fierce dark light. "There was another reason I came back," he said.

She stared at him silently, saying nothing, wanting everything.

"Her name was Meredith Blackmoore. All those years she'd been there, in the back of my mind. A creation of my own imagination? I hoped not. I wanted her to be soft and cool and needy. I wanted her to need me. Do you, Merry? Do you need me?"

She couldn't think for needing him. "Yes," she said.

"Ah," he said, closing his eyes as he pulled away from her. "Merry." Her name was a prayer on his lips. He settled again in his original position, thus shifting her to hers.

She waited.

"I benched those boys," he said.

"I know."

"What'd your parents think?"

"They were upset. Concerned," she amended. "Do you think the boys got the message?"

"I don't know. I hope so. It hurt, you know. I could barely stand seeing them sitting there, watching us lose."

"What will happen if you catch them again?"

He was very still. She could sense his eyes staring into the darkness.

"What are you thinking about, Stoney?"

"I'm thinking about how proud I am of those boys. They're going to win the state championship. I know it. They know it. They're hungry for it. It's in the way their bodies move. In the flash of their eyes.

"What goes on on that field is so clear, so straightforward. No dark secrets there. No unresolved confusion."

"So?" she asked.

"So. You want to know the truth, Meredith? This school hasn't had a state championship in any sport since I left here. And now here I am, the famous soccer player come home to Colton, breathing life into a program that's never enjoyed much popularity in this town. Hell, today I got a call from a national sports magazine."

"You did?"

"It was the third this month. So far, I'm not talking to them, but eventually I'll have to. And then the boys will really get some attention. And pressure. Because I'm here.

"So you ask what will happen if they screw up again? You think I want to pull a kid on this team because he was caught with his hand into something he oughtn't? I'd move heaven and earth not to do that. How many kids have broken the rules over the years? During this year? But how many kids have the chance to say he played on a state-championship team under Stoney Macreay? I don't know what I'd do, Meredith. But I don't want to bench those kids again."

It sounded so logical. Compassionate even. Meredith was actually nodding her head in agreement when she thought of her brother, Roger. It wouldn't help Roger if everyone looked the other way. She thought of Steven and Brett and Roger racing down that highway that night, flirting with disaster and death.

"Your name shouldn't matter," she said tersely. "The publicity shouldn't matter. The game itself shouldn't matter. Those kids know the rules. It's a grown-up world out there, Stoney. If they fool around with grown-up decisions, they ought to have grown-up consequences."

"Right," Stoney said abruptly. "Of course." He slid his body down on the pillows and pulled her with him. "Let's not talk anymore."

"Stoney..."

"The problems will be there tomorrow. I just want you tonight."

As his lips covered hers, and his hands asked questions she was only beginning to understand, she found she was also learning the silent, powerful language of give and take, question and answer. Her hands also performed their own wordless exploration, and her lips made their own hot demands.

Stoney woke the next morning feeling strangely changed, new. He was aware of his own sense of charged expectancy, of almost electrified wonder. Still, he didn't really understand what was truly different until he had showered and dressed and poured himself a cup of instant coffee, and he caught himself humming some silly tune that had been popular years before.

He was *happy.*

Meredith.

Only half knowing what he was doing, he left the kitchen with his cup of coffee, and stood staring at the pillows scattered in front of his fireplace.

She had burned brighter than the fire he'd lit.

So warm, so generous, so... right.

She'd had to leave, of course. Far sooner than he wanted her to, far later than she'd intended.

He'd carried Tess out to the car for Meredith. And dazzled by the light shining from her eyes, he kissed her again in the starlit night. "Mine," he'd whispered, his arms cradling Tess, his mouth owning Meredith.

Mine, he thought now, nursing his coffee, remembering how she'd tasted, how she'd felt.

Still, she had not been all the way his. Not with her daughter sleeping in the same room. They'd both understood the limits set by their sleeping, oblivious chaperone.

Which somehow had made their time together that much more poignant.

And the next time all the more desirable.

He was short of breath even thinking about it.

Ahhh. His sigh was a long, slow sound in his empty room.

He wanted to marry her. He thought she might like to marry him.

And after that, what? What did he have to offer Meredith Blackmoore?

He thought of her business. She'd certainly made a success of it. She was supporting herself and her daughter just fine.

He found himself thinking of his youth. He remembered when he was as young as his players. Soccer had been everything to him then. The sport had always seemed so basic, so wonderfully clean. When he played, he kept his mind on the game and nothing else. When the game was over and his team had won, he basked in the glory of being the star.

The game had given his life a semblance of balance years ago, when everything else had seemed upside down.

And later, after he'd left home, it had been soccer that kept him going, kept him from thinking about things, feeling things, kept him from falling apart. He had literally lived for those minutes on the field, when all he had to think about was moving that black-and-white ball down the field.

It was enough. Until the past couple of years, when those moments of high adrenaline on the field could no longer offset the complexities of his life off it. His personal life had yawned wide in its meaninglessness, and he had to constantly fight feelings of profound loneliness, emptiness, deep-down anger. After a while nothing seemed real to him, not even the game.

So that in an odd but very real sense, his injured knee had almost been a relief.

Until he realized he didn't know anything *except* soccer. When that was gone, who the hell was he?

It was a question he still couldn't answer. He didn't even have a plan for his future.

He thought of his team and the state championship still a month away. He'd give himself until then to come up with some answers. He'd watch his boys win, and then he'd make his plans. And in the meantime there would be Meredith.

Chapter Nine

"Communicate!" Stoney shouted. "Talk to each other!"

Communicating was one of the skills Stoney taught his soccer players, and he knew from experience that it was one of the most important factors in winning a close game. He taught his team to verbalize on the field, calling their moves to each other, congratulating each other as the ball was moved successfully down the field.

The day was heavily overcast. Thick, roiling purple clouds hung threateningly low. The wind blew in hostile waves from the north.

Rain had already fallen earlier in the day; the field was slippery with mud and slick grass. The boys' uniforms bore the results of their slides and falls.

The weather had certainly changed over the past couple of days. The last pleasant night had been the evening he'd held Meredith Blackmoore in his arms.

Too long ago, he thought ruefully. He'd talked with her twice, but she'd resisted seeing him again right away.

There'd been enough time for her to get scared again, he knew.

He really didn't blame her. He'd never known a woman could awaken so beautifully, could unfold so completely. He wondered if she burned at night, thinking about him. He knew he did, thinking about her.

He was thinking about her far too much. Even now, standing on the sidelines, his eyes narrowed in supposed concentration as he watched his team practice, he couldn't get her out of his mind.

Deliberately he shook his head, trying to clear it. The twenty-odd boys on the field were participating in an elaborate dribbling-and-passing drill that he had devised himself. The drill taught speed, accuracy and the aggressiveness necessary to taste the win.

These boys certainly didn't have trouble with that. They were some of the most aggressive young players he'd ever seen. They wanted the championship. And he knew they wanted it not only for themselves. They wanted it for their coach. For Stoney.

They thought he was something, these small-town boys. They were thrilled to have him here.

Frowning suddenly, Stoney watched Bill Parks miss a reception. Bill's face turned suddenly red and angry, and he whirled and raised a fist to the player behind him. Which happened to be Meredith's brother, Roger.

"Hey!" Stoney yelled. "Cut it out, Parks! Communicate! Recover and communicate!"

"Hello, Stoney."

Stoney turned. Mike Callahan had come up behind and was watching the boys, his hands in his pockets. His thick, dark hair was waving in the brisk breeze.

"Hey, Mike."

"How's the team?"

"See for yourself." For a moment they watched the kids in silence—dribble, pass, dribble, pass—keeping the motion constant, fast, smooth.

"So. I saw you with your woman the other night."

His woman. The words tasted so sweet that Stoney was momentarily distracted.

"You look a little silly, Macreay."

"Silly?" He knew Callahan was teasing him. It was probably indicative of his state of mind that he didn't even care.

"Maybe *dazzled* would be a better word. Or *thunderstruck.* Or like maybe you're walking on cloud nine." Mike was laughing openly now.

Stoney grinned. "Shut up, Callahan."

Mike Callahan shifted slightly and raised his hand to shield his eyes as he watched the soccer players practice. "Had any more problems with your players breaking the rules?"

"I don't think so," Stoney replied.

"I think this town is getting pretty excited about this team."

"This team is pretty exciting," Stoney said evenly.

"You think they'll win the championship?" Mike asked.

"Yes," Stoney replied.

"Well. That's what I think, too. So do some other people. Including Dave Pratt. He called me this morning. Said he'd tried to get an interview out of you, but you'd refused. Asked for one from me instead."

Dave Pratt was the leading television sports reporter in the country. "Do as you please," Stoney told Mike.

"Hell," Mike said. "What would I know about talking with somebody like that? I told him it was you or nobody." Mike paused and again watched the boys on the field. "But I got to thinking. With so much curiosity about what's going on here in Colton, what might happen if some of the boys screw up again. What will you do?''

"You think I haven't thought about it? Rules are rules, Callahan.''

"Have you talked with the boys?''

"Some.''

"Do more than some. Tell them I've heard they're partying.''

"Have you?''

Callahan shrugged. "I always hear things. Rarely anything provable. Anyway, talk to your kids. Tell them to lay off, at least until the end of the season. Tell them they've got a national audience. Scare the pants off them. But get them to honor the rules.''

"Sure, boss,'' Stoney said. "The mighty Macreay will personally straighten out every one of those guys.''

Mike snorted. "What about next year, Stoney? What are your plans?''

Stoney had made it clear to Mike that he would only commit to a year of high school coaching. And Mike had never asked for more. Still, Mike's questions made him uncomfortable.

"What *will* you be doing?'' Mike asked again.

"My agent's still active. He'll probably find me some commercials or something. Some shoes to endorse,'' Stoney said.

"You don't sound too thrilled.''

Stoney didn't answer.

"Maybe you ought to find a cause to get involved with,'' Mike suggested. "Lend your name to something useful.''

"Such as?''

"I don't know. Some foundation or other that works with young people. Some inner-city work. Something meaningful.''

Something meaningful. He didn't know if he'd recognize something meaningful if it came up and hit him on the head.

"Something meaningful," Stoney said, almost as if he were experimenting with the word. "Like encouraging kids to stay away from things that are bad for them?" He looked at his watch. Practice time was almost up. Stoney raised his coach's whistle and blew hard. "Right now I've got some boys to flay," he said. "You going to stick around while I lay down the law?"

"No, thanks," Mike said. "But let me know how it goes."

"Right."

As the boys gathered around Stoney, he thought again of Meredith. She'd understand *something meaningful.* He wished he could talk to her about it.

He wished he could talk to her at all.

"What's up, Coach?" Roger Blackmoore queried.

He spread out both arms in a gesture of protection. "Boys, you probably saw Mr. Callahan here, talking with me. He's heard some things. It's time for you and me to have a serious discussion...."

He talked long and hard to his boys, watching their expressions change from assumed innocence to rage to fear. And all the while something else was nagging at him, far in the back of his mind.

Meredith. He missed her already. Not that he didn't understand her hesitancy. Lord knew he was trying to be patient. But waiting was something that had never come naturally to him.

Later, as he watched the now-subdued team leave the field, he decided he'd waited long enough. Whether or not she was ready, he would somehow manage to see Meredith tonight.

He would see her again and feel her again and kiss her again. Until he convinced her of that which he already knew: Meredith Blackmoore was his.

Meredith was working late again. She'd gone home for a quick dinner and an hour with Tess before heading back to the shop.

This afternoon Henry Boles had come bouncing in, full of excitement. "Got it!" he'd shouted, wearing a grin as big as an Indiana cornfield. "Got it! Got it! Got it!" He did a jig around the front office. "Statewide Electric—ten thousand shirts! We have just moved into the big time, Meredith Blackmoore!"

"Ten thousand—" Meredith was astonished.

"Two color. Due four weeks from today. Signed, sealed and delivered." With an excited flourish, Henry waved the signed contract in front of Meredith's face.

"Good Lord," she murmured, staring at her salesman with something approaching awe. She spoke the first thought that came into her head. "Four weeks! But we've already got a month's backlog—"

Henry immediately sobered. "I know it's a challenge, Merry. But it's highly profitable and will lead to even more business. Surely there's a way to get this work done. Hire some more kids or something."

Meredith lowered her eyes to look down at her desk. Henry's suggestion seemed a reasonable one on the surface. She'd already added Beth as part-time help. But in her experience, Beth was the exception. Young people were often unreliable and lacked the perfectionism she demanded. Yet to put more people permanently on the payroll only meant paying unemployment later if she had to lay them off.

If only she loved this work. If only the new business excited her, rather than made her feel so burdened.

Forcing her eyes back up to Henry's now-troubled gaze, she forced a bright smile. "We'll do it somehow," she assured him. "We'll get that work out on time." Then she extended her hand. "Congratulations, Henry."

That had been this afternoon. Now she was here in the office, and it was so late everyone else had finally gone home.

This morning she'd actually done it—she'd contacted a real estate agent specializing in commercial sales. The agent was supposed to have a contract for her to sign tomorrow morning, placing Screens Alive! on the marketplace. And she'd called Purdue for an application.

Yet she knew there was no guarantee the business would sell. Sometimes businesses were on the market for years before a qualified buyer came along.

Nevertheless, it was a first step, she told herself bracingly. She was moving forward in the direction she wanted to go, no matter how slowly. She was going to make her future happen, just as she'd told her father. For the past two days she'd thought with almost fanatical intensity about the future and the plans she needed to make. And with almost the same fierce intensity, she'd tried to avoid thinking about Stoney Macreay.

Once she'd got home the other night, her old insecurities had settled in. She'd never really understood what Tom had really done to her so many years ago. But she knew that her own sense of powerlessness, along with her inability to trust, could be traced to that one horrible night.

Sighing, she turned back to her work. She had a business to run, including ten thousand extra shirts to somehow produce in a month's time. She wouldn't think about Stoney. She wouldn't.

She gave herself a small half smile. As if such a thing were possible.

Nights were the hardest. He was with her in a hundred dreams, a thousand small thoughts. Innumerable fantasies.

The little bell above her shop door jingled. In her distraction she had forgotten to lock it. She looked up to see the object of her thoughts step inside. Stoney Macreay.

Her breath caught in her throat. Her lips curved up in a smile of pure joy before she caught them and forced them straight. Automatically she stood.

Suddenly she no longer felt tired. Or burdened. Or powerless. Suddenly all her impossibilities turned into their opposites.

Stoney was here.

His lion's eyes flamed out, engulfing her in one burningly possessive, all-embracing look. Understanding flickered in his bright depths.

She came around her desk and stretched out her hand in welcome.

"Stoney." Her voice was low, husky, filled with undisguised happiness and longing.

His eyes shuttered, his lips curved slightly upward, he took her hand and pulled her to him. "Maybe now you will talk to me," he said.

"I—"

"You look exhausted," he said.

The tenderness in his tone was almost her undoing, and it was only with the greatest effort that she kept her head upright and her eyes dry. She met his gaze steadily and told him what was most important. "I put the business on the market this morning," she said. "I called Purdue for an application."

His smile was genuine. His eyes were like twin flaming swords, piercing her. "Fine," he said. "Great. I'm proud of you."

"Oh, Stoney," she whispered. "Nothing's fine. Nothing's great." Then she added simply, "I missed you."

All the air went out of him in a giant whoosh. For a moment he stood incredibly still, holding her. Then he wrapped a hand around her head and jerked her forward into his chest. His arms went around her, and he forced her chin up and lowered his head. She barely had time to gasp his name before his lips found hers.

Then there was no more time for thought. Or for worry. Or for dreams that might or might not come true. There was only Stoney, filling her senses, filling her needs. His hands moved up and down her back, hauling her up close, literally lifting her up from the floor. Somehow she had raised one leg and twisted it until it was practically wrapped around his waist. Her mouth was attacking his, her hands were burying themselves in his golden mane, twisting its thickness around her fingers.

He backed her up against a wall and leaned into her, letting her feel his weight, his strength, the long hardness of him.

Neither of them heard the tinkling of the bell above her door. "Meredith, I need to talk to you— Oh! Sorry!"

Stoney slowly lifted his head, shaking it slightly as if reminding himself where he was. Meredith looked around his broad chest to see a red-faced Beth standing in the door.

"I'll leave," Beth offered in obvious embarrassment. "Forget I ever—"

Meredith laid her head against Stoney's heart; she heard it racing madly. She was afraid her face was the same color as Beth's.

In an abrupt motion Stoney removed Meredith's hands from around his neck, shifting both their bodies with graceful control, so that when he was finished his body shielded hers from Beth's widely shocked eyes. "What do you need, Beth?" he said, his tone even and controlled.

"No. It's all right, really. I just wanted to tell Meredith something—"

"You can stay," he said. "I was just leaving."

"Stoney!" Meredith's cry was involuntary.

He turned back to her. "This time *you* call me," he said, his eyes hot with desire, his voice cold with inhuman control.

She felt the blood drain from her face. Her hand went to her heart.

"I can't—" she began.

"You can," he contradicted her with steely sharp softness. "You can do anything you want. You can win any prize you want." He turned to Roger's girlfriend. "See you, Beth. Meredith." He spun on his heel and walked out the door.

Meredith watched him disbelievingly. She walked back to her desk and sat in her chair. She put her face in her hands.

"Merry?" she heard Beth's tentative voice. "Are you all right?"

No, Meredith thought to herself. I'm scared to death. "Sure," she told Beth. She raised her head from her hands and forced a smile. "Come sit by me, Beth. Tell me what you need."

"I really did come at a bad time."

Meredith didn't deny it. "It doesn't matter," she said wearily.

"Are you in love with Coach Macreay?"

In love? With Stoney? She shook her head, trying to block out the joy the thought brought. Surely not. Of course not. She wasn't in love with anybody. How could she be at this time in her life? She had a dream to pursue.

Fear swept through her. She couldn't be in love—that's all. She wouldn't risk it.

"Merry? Do you love him?"

Meredith laughed raggedly. "Of course not."

"You guys looked like you were in love."

"No. This hurts too much to be love." Meredith couldn't believe she'd said that.

"My mother says love hurts sometimes."

Meredith absorbed the secondhand advice. "I would hate to think that's true," she said slowly. "Surely love shouldn't give pain."

"I wouldn't know," Beth said, wide-eyed and solemn. "I don't think I've ever truly been in love."

Meredith stared at her young friend. Just a short time ago Beth had been swearing lasting devotion to Roger. "All right," she said, putting her own confusion aside. "What gives? What's happened now?"

Beth twisted her hands together. She looked down, not meeting Meredith's eyes. "Roger can be such an idiot."

"Umm. Tell me something I don't know."

"All those guys. They're so *stupid*."

"They're stupid," Meredith agreed sagely.

"Just because Coach laid into them today. About their drinking and . . . stuff."

"Coach laid into them?" This was news to Meredith.

"Yeah. I guess he really gave it to them. Told them if anyone was caught again, he'd yank him off the team, no matter who he was or what game was being played. Told them they were all being incredibly dumb. Told them they were losing his respect—that Stoney Macreay's guys never broke training rules, ever."

"Wow," Meredith said, impressed in spite of herself. "They didn't take it so well, huh?"

"To say the least. And Roger least of all."

"What happened?"

Beth became evasive. "Actually I was just on my way home," she said jerkily. "I'm really sorry I interrupted you and Coach. I—I saw your lights and thought I'd stop and use the bathroom. If you don't mind." Beth's chin was high, her voice nervously apologetic. She couldn't seem to meet Meredith's eyes.

Meredith wasn't having any of it. "What *happened?*"

All of a sudden Beth seemed to cave in. She gave a little gulping noise, and the tears started to flow down her cheeks.

"Beth?"

Beth shook her head. "I think I'd better go," she said through her sobs.

"Not on your life," Meredith shot back, quickly coming around her desk to stand between the girl and the door. When she reached out to offer Beth some comfort, Beth jerked away. "Talk to me," Meredith urged. "Tell me what happened."

Again Beth shook her head, burying her head in her hands. "I can't. You'll tell someone. You'll tell Coach. And then Roger will hate me. They all will."

"Tell me, Beth."

Beth slowly lowered her hands and raised her head. "You've got to promise not to tell anyone."

"Not on your life," Meredith repeated grimly. "No promises, Beth. You're just going to have to trust me. You're going to have to trust the fact that I'm your friend." She heard her own words with almost hysterical disbelief. How could she instruct Beth in the nature of trust when she hadn't figured it out herself?

Beth looked almost tragic, standing there against Meredith's office wall. She was wearing a purple blouse, high against her neck. Her shining hair was hanging straight down, and her face was devoid of makeup. She looked impossibly young.

"It's—it's just that nothing's been the same this year. Everything is so different."

"What do you mean?"

Beth glanced away. "The guys. The parties. Everything."

"Everything," Meredith repeated, nodding her head, hoping to get the girl to talk.

"Roger—Roger, he . . ."

"Yes?" Meredith said, going tense.

"He said Coach was right and everyone should go on the wagon."

Relieved, Meredith said, "That's good."

"All the guys were there, and a lot of us girls. And Carl Milson was there."

"Carl Milson doesn't even go to that school anymore," Meredith said slowly. "He graduated two years ago."

"He hangs around, though," Beth said. "He . . . knows about things."

"He deals." Meredith said flatly.

Beth nodded.

"So what happened tonight?"

"The guys were all together, like I said. Somehow Carl found out about it and showed up. He brought some beer, and . . . some other stuff."

"They didn't use tonight, did they?"

Beth paused. "A little. They all did something. Then they told Carl to save the rest for after the season. They told him they'd be ready for him then."

"Good Lord," Meredith murmured.

"Roger wanted more. I told him to hold off, to remember what Coach had said. He really got angry. Some of the other guys told him to chill out. He told me he wanted to take me home. On the way he seemed to go crazy. He stopped the car and he—he tried to . . ."

"Have sex with you?" Meredith said. She sounded cool and calm, but she wasn't. Inside she was hurting, bad. This was *Roger* Beth was talking about. Her little brother.

"I tried to fight him off, Meredith. And I was crying, but he didn't seem to care. Then all of a sudden he stopped and looked at me really strange, as if he didn't even know who I was. Then he hit me. Hard. In my stomach."

"Dear God."

"What's happening to me, Meredith? What's happening to all of us?"

"I've got to tell someone," Meredith said. "This is my brother. I can't keep this a secret."

Beth panicked. "No! You can't do that! You can't!"

Meredith looked straight into Beth's frightened eyes. "Yes, I can," she said evenly. "I'll get you through this, Beth. I won't let anyone hurt you. Not Roger or anyone. But I've got to get help for him. This is my kid brother we're talking about. He was always the boy who would catch the butterflies and then let them go. He couldn't stand to see anything hurt. He needs help. I'm going to make sure he gets it."

"They'll kill me," Beth moaned.

"They're killing themselves," Meredith replied.

Winning was still the thing in Colton. Above all, a kid was a hero if he won.

Meredith knew she should call Stoney. But every time her hand reached for the phone, she remembered him telling her to do just that. When he heard her voice on the line she knew exactly what he'd think.

You can win any prize you want.

She was tired of winning and losing. She was tired of competitions that clouded the issues of right and wrong.

Do you love him? Beth had asked.

She was terrified that she did.

She wanted to talk to Stoney. She wanted to tell him about Beth. And other things. Like maybe he was the one who actually had won. That he was coming perilously close to capturing her heart forever. She hoped her heart was a prize he wanted.

In the meantime this situation with the soccer team had to be dealt with. She wanted Stoney to handle it. She wanted him to believe there were ways to be a hero besides winning a game.

Shoving away her doubts, she picked up the phone and dialed his number. He answered on the first ring. "Meredith." He said her name low and hungry.

"Yes." She found she was breathless, suddenly unable to speak.

"Will you come over? Tonight?"

"Yes."

"Ah."

"There are some things…there is something I need to talk with you about."

"When you get here, there may not be time to talk, lady." He was laughing at her now.

"Stoney?" It was time to fight with the most-powerful weapons she had.

"Yeah."

"I think I'm falling in love with you."

Absolute silence. Happiness such as she had never known exploded within her, battling a sudden fear that had her hands clenching and her stomach tensing nervously. As if from a far distance, she was aware of the clock ticking off long, quiet seconds. Then she heard, "What did you say?"

Maybe she shouldn't have said it. The words certainly hadn't been planned. She felt young and foolish. "Nothing," she said softly. "I didn't say anything."

Another long pause. "All right," she heard him say, very calmly, very precisely. "Just get the hell over here."

"I need to lock up. Then I'll be there."

She was shaking so badly she could hardly hang up the phone. She'd spoken the truth—she really did love him. No matter what else happened, she loved him. It was the strongest feeling she had ever known.

She thought again of Beth, so angry at her, so lost. And Roger, using things he shouldn't, doing things he shouldn't.

In her mind's eye she saw Tess, her daughter. Her child of violence, brought into the world as a mistake, a fatherless bastard. Yet no one was happier than Tess.

Except Meredith, at this moment. Love really does make life possible, she thought to herself wonderingly. In spite of everything, love survives.

She shut off the lights, locked the door and walked out on the work behind her. She got in her car and drove to Stoney's.

"Come on in," Stoney called in response to her knock, his muffled voice wickedly, deliciously sardonic. Feeling suddenly unsure, Meredith turned the knob and went inside his house.

He was waiting for her, much as he had the other night, sunk down into his easy chair. His feet were stretched out and crossed at his ankles, his heels resting in deceptive nonchalance on his coffee table. His arms were folded behind his head.

His house was filled with shadows. Stoney had lit only the small lamp that rested on the table next to his chair. Its insufficient light pooled downward from the side of his head to his feet. She could not see his eyes. Yet she knew he was staring at her. She felt insecure in the darkness, pierced by things she could barely understand.

"Come here," he said.

The peace she had felt in the car left her; she felt a fierce desire to flee.

"Hello, Stoney," she said uncertainly.

"Take it off," he nodded at the light winter coat she was wearing, "and come here."

There was a closet by the door. Silently, her chin up and her hands steady, she peeled off her coat and hung it on a hanger. Then she turned and walked into his living room.

She could see him better now. He was golden, sitting there in his circle of imperfect light. His eyes were the color of a storm, wild and wary and untamed.

She sat down in a side chair at right angles to his. "Stoney—" She said his name with uncertainty.

"Say it again," he ordered softly. "What you said on the phone."

She closed her eyes. She found she had no voice.

"Please," he said "Say it again."

"I—I think I'm falling in love with you, Stoney."

His body shifted. He threw his head back against the chair and stared at the ceiling. When he spoke his voice was very low. "Thank you." Then he added unsmilingly, "I think I'm falling in love with you, too."

She made a little sound in her throat. She closed her eyes. She felt unexpectedly like crying.

"I don't know who I am," Stoney said. "I don't know what I'll be. But I want to marry you, Meredith."

"Oh, Stoney," she said. "I don't know if—"

"Don't give me the reasons why not, Merry. There are a thousand reasons why not. And only one or two reasons why. But they're the most important reasons of all."

"I want to go to school—"

"Of course," he said, "Although some time I'd like you to have my baby, Meredith."

Stoney's baby. Stoney and her, making it. Stoney and her, raising it.

Her heart constricted in her chest.

She thought of Tess. Tess would no doubt adore a baby brother or sister—that was no risk. No, it was the memory of Tess growing up without a father, loving her secret gifts, never really understanding what she was missing.

Tess would also be their baby.

As if reading her mind, Stoney said, "I'll love Tess, Meredith."

The slow tears began their painstaking course down her cheeks.

Stoney's eyes, which had been closed, opened. They were very dark. He leaned forward so that his elbows were on his knees. The shadows emphasized the sculpted planes of his face.

"I want to touch you." His voice was hoarse. He stood up and held out his hand. She took it, knowing he felt her slight trembling. He tugged, and she also stood. He cupped her face with both his hands. "You are so beautiful," he said.

She felt his fingers tighten almost bruisingly along her cheekbone. His lips brushed hers, once, twice, a third time. She realized he was shaking with desire.

For her. He desired her. She still couldn't get used to it—this great gift.

"Stoney," she murmured, a rush of emotion sweeping through her. "I love you so much, Stoney."

He went still, then, in that way he had of holding things in. He leaned his forehead against the top of her head. Automatically her arms moved to surround his waist; his did the same.

They stood that way for an endless silent moment before, with a groan of pleasure, he took her mouth in one hot, long, rough kiss of victorious possession. Before he was done, she was sagging against him in mindless delight. His lips left her mouth to leave a flaming trail across her temple, lighting fires in the soft virgin folds of her ears, planting passion in the tender, incredibly responsive hollows of her neck.

She had thought he had kissed her before; she had thought he had awakened her before.

"Stoney," she whispered. "I didn't think anyone could ever want me this much, could make me feel this much...."

"I'll always want you," he told her. "This is forever, Meredith."

"Yes," she agreed, feeling radiant.

He looked at her as if he could eat her alive. Then, shaking his head like a jungle animal being roused from a deep sleep, he turned from her to pour a single glass of wine from his kitchen.

"Aren't you going to have some?" she asked as he handed the glass to her.

"No. My boys are in season. For the time being I follow the same rules they do."

As if from a far distance she remembered her conversation with Beth. "Then you might as well drink some wine, Stoney," she said slowly.

"What?"

"Beth told me some things tonight. I'd better share them with you." She related everything Beth had told her.

At first Stoney didn't respond. His arm was around her shoulder, his hand bent into a loose fist so that his knuckles brushed her cheek.

"Stoney?"

"Dammit, Meredith. Those boys can win that championship."

"Right," she said. When he said nothing, she asked, "So what will you do?"

"Hell. It should be an easy call, right?"

"Well, I think so, Stoney. But I've never been vested in winning like some people I know."

"That's not the only thing, Merry. I was putting off making my own nebulous plans until that crown was won."

She thought he was teasing her in order to avoid the more serious issue. She played along. "So what do you have in mind to be when you grow up?"

Stoney shrugged. His eyes were closed. "I'm reviewing my options," he said.

"Such as?"

"Can't play soccer—that's out. I don't really want to continue to coach. Not as the main activity of my life anyway. I could do commercials and endorsements for a few years, if I didn't find the idea so abhorrent."

"So what's left?"

"I could invest my money and watch it grow."

"Come on, Stoney. If you could do anything in the world you wanted to do, what would it be?"

It took a moment for him to answer, so that she knew he was thinking something through, that finally he was going to say something that mattered.

"I'd like to work with kids," he said, in the low, flat voice that told her more than he knew. "Coaching problem kids. Or maybe not even coaching. I'd just like to do whatever I could. Wherever I could. I'd like to help."

She smiled, in spite of everything feeling her love for him grow even larger. "You'll find a way," she told him. "I believe in you."

"Enough to marry me? You haven't answered me yet."

Sometime that evening she'd made up her mind. "Yes," she said. "Enough to marry you, Stoney."

He never looked more beautiful to her than he did at that moment, when his eyes changed slowly from almost a diffident humility to something approaching awe. He didn't say anything at all. He just wrapped his arms around her and pulled her close against his chest. Then, some minutes later he spoke her name very softly into her hair. "Merry."

That was all. It was enough.

Chapter Ten

The next morning Stoney went to see his friend, Colton High's athletic director, Mike Callahan. Though he and Meredith hadn't spent a lot of time talking about Roger and the rest of the team last night, Stoney knew he would lose Meredith's respect if he didn't do something pretty fast. She was more than a little upset about Roger and his no-doubt drug-induced attack on Beth. It was a miracle Beth had not been hurt more than she was.

He still couldn't believe his boys had used drugs last night, within hours of his fierce scolding. And even if they planned for their partying activities to be over until after the season, they had played by their own rules, not the game's.

Stoney was furious.

They had a game scheduled for that very evening. When Stoney got to the high school, he saw posters on the walls and windows, and winced. Stoney's Boys Are Number One, some read. Others said Good Luck To Stoney's Boys.

Stoney's boys had screwed up good.

He found Mike in his office, talking to a man and a woman Stoney knew only too well. Mike stood when he saw Stoney, and grinned with relief. "Stoney. You know Luke Matthias and Susan Davidson. From *American Sports Magazine*. They want to do an article on the team."

"Hey, Macreay," Luke said. "Long time no see. How's your knee?"

"Fine," Stoney said. Luke was one of the best sportswriters in the country. Over the years Stoney had spoken with him several times. He looked at the woman. "How are you, Susan?"

She gave him her professionally ingratiating smile. "I'd be better if we could just talk the two of you into cooperating with us on this article. We plan to make it our lead in December. We'd like to talk in depth about small-town sports, and we thought the best way would be to follow your team from here on out to the state championship." She gave a delicate pause, then appealed to his old winning instincts. "You are going to take the state crown, aren't you, Stoney?"

He forced himself to relax, to sound fresh, almost cocky. "You got a tape recorder going here? Has the interview started already?"

Still smiling, she said, "Of course not, Stoney."

Susan was smiling. Luke was smiling. Mike Callahan was smiling. And Stoney himself was smiling.

One smiling crew, he told himself. Only none of us is going to get what we really want. "How about you let Mike and me talk for a few minutes?" he suggested.

"Of course," Luke said. "Sure," Susan added. They left Mike's office, shutting the door gently behind them.

"Well, Stoney. We might as well say yes. With all the calls I've been getting, you're going to have to accept the publicity sometime. You might as well pick your medium.''

"You never really pick your medium with the press,'' Stoney corrected him. "I'm afraid this would only be the beginning. Before you know it, we'd have television and radio people here, and other print reporters. If there were going to be a story. Which there isn't, Mike.''

Mike sat down, eyeing Stoney warily. "No story?'' he questioned. "What do you mean?''

"I'm going to pull my team from competition,'' Stoney said flatly.

"What?"

In as few words as possible, Stoney explained to Mike what Meredith had told him yesterday. Halfway through the story, Mike started to shake his head. "Don't do this, Stoney,'' he said. "They've made a pact not to break rules again until the season is over. What will it help to tear everything apart now? Let those boys have their moment of glory. Pretend that Meredith never told you anything. Pretend you don't know anything.''

"I wish I could,'' Stoney said wearily. He didn't add that Meredith would never let him pretend. Nor would his own conscience.

"What about those reporters out there? If they get wind of this, they could make our little soccer team a national story. What will *that* do to our boys?''

"I don't know,'' Stoney admitted. "I only know what I have to do. Let the consequence follow, whatever it may be.''

Mike was not appeased. Stoney watched as his ashen-faced friend asked Luke Matthias and Susan Davidson to leave. Trying to sound unconcerned, he told them that he and Stoney had decided a national story was not in the team's best interest. Then he pulled Stoney back into his office and argued with him for over an hour. Finally Mike admitted defeat. "All right,'' he agreed reluctantly. "We'd better get those parents on the phone. We'd better call a meeting. But you do the talking, Stoney. I'll be there to support you, but you do the talking."

The meeting was called for immediately after school, during normal practice time. Stoney had called Meredith and asked her to come, too. The school secretary spent the afternoon calling team members' parents. As the young men gathered in the library, the sight of the group of parents sitting there seemed to fill them with dismay. The school principal and superintendent were also present. A sense of foreboding filled the room. Everyone seemed to understand that something serious was wrong.

Meredith sat in the back of the room, watching Stoney. Her mother was there, but her father had not been able to make it. Stoney seemed relaxed but solemn.

After everyone had a chance to find a seat, Stoney began. What he had to say didn't take long. In precise, clipped language he laid out exactly what he knew. He told the stunned, silent group that he was disqualifying the team from further play, and he was making a public announcement as to why. The boys grew sullen, then mad and then, like very small boys who had lost the prize, many of them began to cry. In their minds they had already won the state crown.

Now it was lost to them forever.

The parents were worse. An unbelievable number of them blamed Stoney, and he stood silent while they railed at him in front of their boys.

By seven o'clock that evening all of Colton knew the truth. Stoney Macreay had blown the whistle on his team.

There would be no soccer game that evening. There would be no more soccer games that season. The first state championship Colton would have had in years had just disappeared in one coach's decision to hold his team accountable to the rules.

Stoney Macreay was not a popular man.

* * *

Meredith stayed by Stoney's side during that long, terrible day. She watched as the local television station interviewed the man she had so recently learned to love. "There are more important things than winning and losing," he said to the television audience. "The boys knew the rules. They broke them. They were given a second chance. They broke them again. It's important that those of us who set the rules believe in what we did, and it's important that we don't waver now, no matter how important the sport or what our chances of winning are."

Maybe his comment would have stayed mainly in Colton, except Luke Matthias and Susan Davidson were still in town. Before the night was out, his television clip was being played on the national networks, and morning newspapers all over the country carried pictures of Stoney Macreay with Meredith by his side.

In Colton there was anger in the stores and businesses, in the living rooms and kitchens. Instead of the Colton soccer team being the budding town heroes, they were now a national disgrace. Yet most people figured those boys were just doing what boys everywhere did—why make them the scapegoats? Why bring down the entire town?

Many of the people of Colton blamed the new antihero, Stoney Macreay.

Meredith knew it bothered Stoney more than he was showing. He had really loved those boys. *His team. His boys.* She sat with him in his living room while his phone rang and rang. He answered every call, explaining with inhuman patience why he'd done what he'd done. She could hear people shouting at him profanely through the receiver—the players' parents, the townspeople, other young friends of the team. "I just wanted to mean something to those guys," he told her during a lull. "My never-ending quest to be a hero has once again ended in a farce. What a joke."

"You're my hero," she told him urgently.

He pulled her close. For a long moment he held her silently. Then he shook his head. "I'm nobody's hero," he told her harshly. "Not my family's. Not my sister's. Not my team's. Not this town's."

"It wasn't your fault," she told him. "Those kids knew what they were doing. You're blaming yourself for doing the right thing."

"Was it the right thing, Meredith?"

"You bet," she told him firmly.

"Your brother was crying. *Crying.*"

"He *hit* Beth. Roger—gentle, quiet, loving Roger—*hit* his girlfriend. Letting him continue would have been wrong, Stoney. *You did the right thing.*"

Someone was knocking on Stoney's door. "Oh, God," he muttered. "What now?"

"Meredith? Stoney? Are you in there?" It was her father.

Immediately Meredith rose and went to the door. Both her mother and father were standing there. "Hi, Daddy. Mom," she greeted them seriously.

Her father said, "We need to talk with Stoney."

"Come on in," Stoney said, standing. He extended his hand. "Hello, Mr. Blackmoore. Mrs. Blackmoore."

For a minute Meredith's parents stood staring at them both. Meredith moved closer to Stoney, her hand reaching out to find his. Hudson's eyes narrowed. "Can we sit down?" he asked quietly.

"Of course," Stoney said. Meredith sat with him on his sofa; her father took an easy chair, and Meredith's mom a side chair. Meredith remembered another time, years ago, when her father and mother had sat facing other members of Stoney's family. She hoped her parents realized how different this was.

"We've come about Roger," Hudson said without preamble. "Is it true he was participating in the things that got the team axed? Was he a part of what was going on?"

Stoney glanced at Meredith. "I'm afraid so," he said awkwardly.

"What exactly has been going on?" her mom repeated.

Squeezing Stoney's hand, Meredith answered for him. "The entire team has been involved in some big-time partying. Roger's been doing things for at least a year. Beth tells me he's frequently out of control."

"Frequently?" her mother whispered.

"Mom. Dad. This is going to be hard to say. I've known some things for a while. I should have told you sooner. But better late than never, I guess." And starting with the conversation she'd had with Beth on their Sunday walk, Meredith outlined for her parents what she knew. But telling them that Roger had actually hit Beth was the hardest of all.

"Roger?" Kathleen Hudson said disbelievingly. "Roger struck a girl? He hit Beth Pierson?"

"I'm afraid so," Meredith said. "I'm really sorry."

She thought her mother wanted to cry. She'd never seen her dad look so bleakly stern. "I think we'd better talk with Beth's parents," he said slowly. "I think we'd better find out more about what's been happening in our children's lives." He looked at Stoney. "What you did today took courage, son. Not to mention a firm sense of right and wrong. Thank you."

Stoney looked startled. A small smile crept across his face. "Thanks," he said. "I needed that more than you know. Not everyone has been so...understanding. Although I must say, I haven't always understood what's right and what's wrong myself." Meredith's hand was still entwined with Stoney's.

"Just so you understand it when it comes to my daughter," Hudson said.

Meredith blushed. "Daddy—"

"I'm going to marry her," Stoney said.

Meredith's mother's eyes widened. "Merry," she said. "You two are going to get married! Does Tess know?"

"Not yet. We haven't known for so long ourselves."

Hudson had yet to smile. "Meredith, do you love this man?"

It was the one question she felt good about answering. It was strange, to know something with such exquisite certainty. "Yes," she said luminously. "Oh yes, Dad."

"And does he love you?"

Stoney answered for himself. "Yes," he said. "With all my heart."

"Well, then," Hudson said, "Something good has come of this mess. Welcome to our family, Stoney. Congratulations to you both."

And Kathleen Blackmoore burst into tears.

Quickly Meredith left her seat by Stoney's side and knelt by her mother, putting her arms around her mother's waist. "Mom," she said. "I'm so sorry, Mom."

"You? What do you have to be sorry for?" her mother said.

"We haven't been easy to raise, have we? Roger and me? It seems like between the two of us we've made every mistake in the book."

But her mother shook her head, stopping her flow of tears. "We didn't ask for easy," she said. "Only possible. But it's a different world out there than when I was growing up. I didn't know, maybe I didn't want to know. I should have prepared you better, protected you more."

"Mom. What could you have done that you haven't already? You gave us time and love and value. It's not your fault."

They hugged each other tight. "Don't forget," her mother said, "your father and I also love you and Tess. With all our hearts."

"I know, Mom," Meredith said. "Don't worry. Everything's going to be all right."

Meredith thought again about the soccer team. For such a short time they had been the recognized heroes in this town. But maybe the true heroes were the unrecognized ones—the mothers and fathers who raised their children with hope, in spite of everything. The ones who taught by their own strength what it was to be strong.

Meredith hoped she and Stoney could be parents like that. She knew that they would try.

A week later Stoney was sitting with Meredith in the hanging swing on her parents' front porch. It had been an eventful seven days, starting with Stoney and her telling Tess that they were going to get married.

"You are!" Tess had exclaimed. "You're going to get married? Coach is going to be my dad? You're kidding! Oh boy!" She had danced in exuberant circles for at least fifteen minutes. "This is the happiest moment of my life!"

Meredith, who knew her daughter well, merely smiled with serene indulgence. Until she glanced at Stoney and saw him watching her daughter with unbelieving awe. His eyes blinked. She realized, disbelieving, that he was holding back tears.

Impulsively she kissed him fully on his mouth.

"Mom!" Tess said, running up to them breathlessly. "Are you kissing again? How come you have to do that so many times?"

"Because, honey," Meredith replied cheekily, "a woman always kisses her hero."

"Oh," Tess said, and kissed Stoney, too.

Now, sitting on the swing, Meredith realized that that had been one of the best things that had happened this week. Some of the other events had been less than pleasant.

Meredith's father called a substance-abuse treatment center, making an appointment for a very angry and very scared Roger. He had been sullen and hateful to Meredith and Stoney since then.

And the controversy in the town was still going strong.

As if reading her mind, Stoney said, "This town will hate me forever, I think."

She shook her head. "You were an easy target. They're getting over it. There's been some letters in the paper, praising what you did."

"It was hard, you know."

She smiled wryly. "I *was* there, Stoney."

"You think I did the right thing."

"Of course. A few of the boys came by the shop today," she told him. "From the team. They want to talk to you. They think *you* hate them."

"I don't."

"I know, Stoney. Some of those guys may never forgive you or figure out exactly why you did what you did. But others—they'll need your understanding. Now more than ever."

He kissed her head in acknowledgment of her words.

Just then a brown sedan pulled up in front of the Blackmoore home. A businesslike woman in her midfifties got out and headed up the steps.

"Oh, no," Stoney murmured, stiffening in anger. "Not another reporter."

"Miranda George," the woman introduced herself. "Are you Stoney Macreay?"

"Yes," Stoney said tersely.

"I've come a long way to see you, Mr. Macreay. I'm with a group of parents who are organizing a congressional lobbying group called ACST, or the Association for Clean and Sober Teens. We wondered if you would like to be involved in what we're doing...."

Beside her Meredith could feel Stoney go very still. "Excuse me?" he queried softly.

Miranda George looked a little uncertain. "I've come from Washington," she said. "Actually I've been in Indianapolis talking with some of the people from your state. We thought you might be interested..."

"Something meaningful," Meredith heard Stoney mutter under his breath. He stood up. "Yes," he said. "I'd be interested." He looked at Meredith. "Do you think your parents would mind if we used their living room?"

"Of course not," she said. "Won't you come in, Miss George?"

The state-championship game was played a month later. Nobody from Colton was there. When it was finally over and the winner announced, people seemed to settle down a little, let go of some of their anger. Some people even began to have second thoughts. Especially in light of some very public statements that were being made in other places. Some very big-name athletes from various sports had spoken on Stoney's behalf. And some politicians had. The state governor had.

Stoney and Meredith were married between Christmas and New Year's, in a very small, very private ceremony in the Blackmoores' living room. Meredith closed Screens Alive! for a week, and she and Stoney honeymooned in the Bahamas. But the best part was coming home, lying in the dark in Stoney's bedroom, with Tess in the room next door, and knowing this closeness was how it was going to be for the rest of her life.

They stayed in Colton for almost a year, until Meredith's business finally sold. The organization Stoney had joined grew to over a thousand members its first year. Much of the work for ACST could be done right out of their home, though sometimes he traveled to make speeches in Washington and other places, and sometimes he helped organize local chapters. Whenever he could, he spoke directly to middle and high school students, urging them to stay strong and straight. Often Meredith and Tess went with him.

Colton's anger at Stoney had been fierce and communal. The apologies came in one by one, in the form of letters, phone calls, visits. The boys on the team came to see him, singly, in pairs. Two or three never forgave him at all.

Roger completed his treatment and came home. It wasn't long, though, before he relapsed, and at the end of the year he was back in the treatment center, trying again. It would be two more years and one more stay in the hospital before Roger and his family could even begin to think with hope about his future.

Meredith's business sold the following October. She didn't enter college until the next fall, when she enrolled at Purdue, just as she'd planned. In the years following she pursued her dream, getting her degree, then going on to medical school. She graduated at the top of her class, and served as a fine physician for the rest of her life. During the years of her education she had two children—a boy and another girl. The boy was planned—he came in late June, during summer break. The girl, however, came right before Christmas one year, in the middle of finals. They named her Barbara.

Stoney's work with substance abuse and teen athletes became well-known all throughout the state of Indiana. In time he was asked to serve on a national president's commission, and acted in that capacity for over two decades. He became, for many, a symbol of all that was meaningful, true and good in the world.

Through the years, at the end of their busy days, they'd curl into each other in the warm darkness of their bed. Meredith would reach up and touch his lips.

"My hero," she'd whisper. "My love."

*　*　*　*　*

In July, get to know the Fortune family....

Next month, don't miss the start of Fortune's Children, a fabulous new twelve-book series from Silhouette Books.

Meet the Fortunes—a family whose legacy is greater than riches. Because where there's a will...there's a wedding!

When Kate Fortune's plane crashes in the jungle, her family believes that she's dead. And when her will is read, they discover that Kate's plans for their lives are more interesting than they'd ever suspected.

Look for the first book, *Hired Husband*, by *New York Times* bestselling author **Rebecca Brandewyne**. PLUS, a stunning, perforated bookmark is affixed to *Hired Husband* (and selected other titles in the series), providing a convenient checklist for all twelve titles!

FREE
Keepsake
Bookmark

Launching in July wherever books are sold.

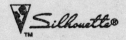

MILLION DOLLAR SWEEPSTAKES
AND EXTRA BONUS PRIZE DRAWING

SWP-ME96

SOMETIMES BIG SURPRISES
COME IN SMALL PACKAGES!

AN UNEXPECTED DELIVERY
by Laurie Paige

Any-minute-mom-to-be Stacey Gardenas was snowbound at
her boss's cabin—without a hospital or future husband in
sight! That meant handsome, hard-nosed Gareth Clelland
had to deliver the baby himself. With the newborn cradled
in his arms, Garth was acting like a proud new daddy—and
that had Stacey hoping for an unexpected proposal!

Coming in May from

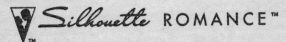

This July, watch for the delivery of...

An exciting new miniseries that appears in a different Silhouette series each month. It's about love, marriage—and Daddy's unexpected need for a baby carriage!

Daddy Knows Last unites five of your favorite authors as they weave five connected stories about baby fever in New Hope, Texas.

- **THE BABY NOTION** by Dixie Browning
  (SD#1011, 7/96)

- **BABY IN A BASKET** by Helen R. Myers
  (SR#1169, 8/96)

- **MARRIED...WITH TWINS!**
  by Jennifer Mikels
  (SSE#1054, 9/96)

- **HOW TO HOOK A HUSBAND (AND A BABY)**
  by Carolyn Zane
  (YT#29, 10/96)

- **DISCOVERED: DADDY** by Marilyn Pappano
  (IM#746, 11/96)

Daddy Knows Last arrives in July...only from

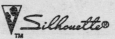

DKLT

What do women really want to know?

Trust the world's largest publisher of women's fiction to tell you.

HARLEQUIN ULTIMATE GUIDES™

I CAN FIX THAT

A Guide For Women
Who Want To Do It Themselves

This is the only guide a self-reliant woman will ever need to deal with those pesky items that break, wear out or just don't work anymore. Chock-full of friendly advice and straightforward, step-by-step solutions to the trials of everyday life in our gadget-oriented world! So, don't just sit there wondering how to fix the VCR—run to your nearest bookstore for your copy now!

Available this May, at your favorite retail outlet.

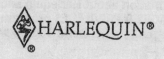

HARLEQUIN®

You're About to Become a *Privileged Woman*

Reap the rewards of fabulous free gifts and benefits with proofs-of-purchase from Silhouette and Harlequin books

Pages & Privileges™

It's our way of thanking you for buying our books at your favorite retail stores.

Pages & Privileges ™

Harlequin and Silhouette—
the most privileged readers in the world!

For more information about Harlequin and Silhouette's PAGES & PRIVILEGES program call the Pages & Privileges Benefits Desk: 1-503-794-2499

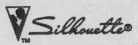

Silhouette®

SR-PP130